THE WORLD'S WEIRDEST NEWS STORIES

JOHN A. TORRES
EDITED BY TIM HEALEY

MAKING HEADLINES

Enslow Publishing
101 W. 23rd Street
Suite 240
New York, NY 10011
USA
enslow.com

This edition published in 2017 by Enslow Publishing, LLC.
101 W. 23rd Street, Suite 240, New York, NY 10011

Library of Congress Cataloging-in-Publication Data

Names: Torres, John.
Title: The world›s weirdest news stories / John Torres and Tim Healey.
Description: New York : Enslow Publishing, 2017. | Series: Making headlines | Includes index.
Identifiers: ISBN 9780766083776 (library bound)
Subjects: LCSH: Curiosities and wonders—Juvenile literature.
Classification: LCC AG243.T67 2017 | DDC 031.02—dc23

Printed in China

To Our Readers: We have done our best to make sure all website addresses in this book were active and appropriate when we went to press. However, the author and the publisher have no control over and assume no liability for the material available on those websites or on any websites they may link to. Any comments or suggestions can be sent by e-mail to customerservice@enslow.com.

Photo Credits: Cover, pp. 1, 18 Beso Gulashvili/AFP/Getty Images; pp. 6–7 Lenscap Photography/Shutterstock.com; p. 10 Scott E Read/Shutterstock.com; p. 16 Inti Ocon/AFP/Getty Images; p. 27 Eric Chuang/Photodics/Getty Images; p. 34 Ricardo Saraiva/Shutterstock.com; p. 42 © ILN/Mary Evans/The Image Works; p. 46 Library of Congress/Corbis Historical/Getty Images; p. 51 Sankei Archive/Getty Images; p. 62 Barcroft Media/Getty Images; p. 66 Colin Davey/Hulton Archive/Getty Images; p. 76 Hulton Archive/Archive Photos/Getty Image; p. 78 Topical Press Agency/Hulton Archive/Getty Images; p. 84 Bettmann/Getty Images; pp. 91, 131, 138 © AP Images; p. 95 Boston Globe/Getty Images; p. 99 fStop Images - Caspar Benson/Brand X Pictures/Getty Images; p. 110 Brian Kinney/Shutterstock.com; p. 119 © Fortean/TopFoto/The Image Works; p. 127 Eryk Fitkau/Photographer's Choice/Getty Images; p. 143 Universal Images Group/Getty Images; p. 147 ullstein bild/Getty Images; p. 153 Rolls Press/Popperfoto/Getty Images; cover (inset), pp. 9, 26, 41, 61, 75, 86, 108, 125, 142, 157, 158, 159 © iStockphoto.com/Maxiphoto; pp. 12, 28, 55, 69, 82, 89, 112, 134, 150 (map) twobee/Shutterstock.com.

CONTENTS

Acknowledgments

The bulk of this book was compiled from newspaper reports consulted at the Bodleian Library in Oxford and the British Museum Newspaper Library in Colindale. I am grateful to the staff of both for their uncomplaining efforts in dealing with some very heavy volumes. Additionally, I have used my own files of offbeat newspaper clippings.

It is not possible to catalog here all of the newspapers referred to. Listed alphabetically, the main present-day publications include: the *Daily Express*, the *Daily Mail*, the *Daily Mirror*, the *Daily Telegraph*, the *Guardian*, the *Illustrated London News*, *Nature*, *New Scientist*, the *News of the World*, *Newsweek*, the *New York Times*, the *Observer*, the *Scientific American*, the *Sun*, the *Sunday Express*, the *Sunday Mirror*, the *Sunday People*, the *Sunday Telegraph*, the *Sunday Times*, *Time*, the *Times,* and the *Washington Post*. I have found the annual index to the *Times* an especially fruitful starting point for research.

I have traced a few of the accounts through Christopher Logue's *Bumper Book of True Stories* (Private Eye Publications) and also obtained newspaper references from Francis Hitching's *The World Atlas of Mysteries* (Collins, 1978) and Peter Haining's *Ancient Mysteries* (Sidgwick and Jackson, 1977).

I have consulted the *Guinness Book of Records* for some background material and used other books for the same purpose, notably: Charles Fort's *The Book of the Damned* (Abacus, 1973), Angus Hall's *Strange Cults* (Aldus/Jupiter, 1976), E. S. Turner's *The Shocking History of Advertising!* (Ballantine, 1952), *Patent Applied For*, by Coppersmith and Lynx (Co-ordination, 1949), and J.S. Curl's *The Victorian Celebration of Death* (David and Charles, 1972).

Finally, I have included some newspaper extracts contained in the following excellent anthologies: H. L. Mencken's *Americana* (Hopkinson, 1925, 1926), George Ives's *Man*

Bites Man (Penguin, 1981), and *This England*, edited by Michael Bateman (Penguin, 1969).

Tim

Additional sources used in this edition:

Associated Press. "Buzz of Buzzards: Bridgewater hangs dead birds to scare off live ones." NJ.com, March 12, 2013. http://www.nj.com/passaic-county/index.ssf/2013/03/buzz_off_buzzards_bridgewater_hangs_dead_birds_to_scare_off_the_living_ones.html.

"Farmer bites cobra to death in Nepal." BBC News, Auguat 23, 2012. http://www.bbc.com/news/world-asia-19348834.

It seems that the public has an insatiable appetite for news, particularly strange and unusual news stories.

INTRODUCTION

Just the other morning, while enjoying my morning coffee before heading off to the newspaper where I work as the news columnist, a headline from the *Huffington Post* caught my eye. It read: "Stray cat gives birth to extremely rare werewolf kitten."

Knowing that werewolves exist only in Eastern European folklore and horror movie sets—don't tell all the "Team Jacob" Twilight fans—it was a story I just had to click and read. Why? Well, just about every journalism student in history—or every journalist for that matter—has asked time after time: What stories or events constitute news?

One of my journalism teachers at New York's Fordham University answered that question with the patented standing reply: "When a dog bites a man," he said, "that is not news. But if a man bites a dog, well, then that is definitely news."

That being said, with the power of social media, instant videos, and live streaming, the competition to find the most unique stories is fierce among news gatherers. The more salacious or intriguing the headline, then the more likely someone will "click" on the story. Newspapers used to set advertising rates by the number of copies they sold. Now it is based on the number of clicks generated on the website.

So, back to the stray cat giving birth to a werewolf story.

Well, it wasn't quite the man changes to wolf under a full moon story I was hoping for. Instead it was about a weird and rare mutation—a wolf cat or Lykoi cat—that results in, well, let's just say a very strange-looking kitty.

Who among us has not gaped at the newsstands in the supermarket to marvel at the headlines announcing that Elvis was abducted by Martians or a woman has given birth to a fish boy? We live in the real, sometimes mundane world, and we want something new, something different to catch and hold our attention.

We want the world's weirdest news stories.

CHAPTER ONE: ANIMAL CRACKERS

Almost Human

On June 2, 1971, newspapers reported that Iris the Elephant, of the Twycross Zoo in England, had learned to play "When the Saints Go Marching In" on a harmonica.

The achievements of animals have always exerted a powerful fascination in humans, and snippets concerning their exploits have long been the staple diet of newspaper readers. Dogs and cats with a special love of Mozart, or of some TV jingle, are so often reported that they scarcely deserve a mention. A more offbeat case was described by the *Times* of August 21, 1982, concerning a musical otter with a particular fondness for the French horn. Whenever musician Henry Merlen practiced his horn on the bank of a stream, it appears, the otter swam toward him, climbed onto a platform of weeds, and sat bolt upright to listen intently to bits of Beethoven.

Of course, with Internet sites like YouTube, animal hijinks or hidden talents become viral news stories overnight. Who hasn't rocked to the groovy moves of "Keyboard Cat," or tried to find some semblance of a smile in "Grumpy Cat?"

Of course, one cannot expect animals to be perfect; they share our weaknesses as well as our strengths. Particularly distressing is their habit of going around stark naked; more than one fastidious eccentric has tried to encourage owners to clothe their pets for the sake of decency. And some animals are frankly unsavory in their appearance and habits. In the United States in 1925, the *Yankton Press* noted: "Legislators

In Germany, a bear was brought to trial for frightening local villagers. Local officials had trouble finding a jury of his peers.

gathering here have received word that a representative of the National Association for the Improvement of the Appearance of Hogs will urge that the appearance of swine should be uniform and artistic."

Unsightliness, of course, is only a minor misdemeanor. In more serious cases, animals have actually been brought before the courts. Animal trials have a long pedigree. In 1499, for example, a German bear was brought to trial for terrorizing villages; through a legal nicety, the case was delayed for several days on a plea that the bear had a right to be tried by a jury of fellow bears. In Switzerland in 1906, a dog was tried and condemned to death for participating in a murder (its human accomplices, two brothers, were sentenced to life imprisonment). In Libya in 1974, a dog was tried for biting a human being and sentenced to a month's imprisonment on a diet of bread and water. Seriously. Some, however, impose their own brand of justice. In 2012, A Nepali rice farmer grabbed the cobra that had just bit him and returned the favor over and over until the snake died.

Often, though, animals are forgiven for their failings, and people have gone to extraordinary lengths to protect them when danger threatens. Firemen have been known to give mouth-to-mouth resuscitation to animals, and in recent years we have seen images on the nightly news of animals wearing oxygen masks after being exposed to smoke.

A breathless report was filed in June 1980, following a production of a play that required a live goldfish in its bowl be dashed to the floor onstage. Hardly had the infamous act been accomplished than an RSPCA inspector rushed from his seat, jumped on stage, and rescued the gasping creature by popping it into a water-filled plastic bag. He had come prepared. The goldfish survived and became the centerpiece of an important legal case. In London, two High Court judges ruled that a goldfish was a captive animal and entitled to the law's protection under the 1911 Protection of Animals Act.

If care is lavished on goldfish, what love is expended on dolphins, those most enchanting and intelligent of creatures? Apart from their exhilarating feats of leaping and retrieval, dolphins have been taught the elements of true communication with humans, doing passable impressions of singing and laughter. Their own vocabulary consists of at least thirty-two distinct sounds. A dolphin's brain is as large as a human's; it has even been established that the creatures get ulcers when anxious. If any animal deserves the description "almost human," it is surely the noble dolphin. Small wonder, that when a 350-pound (158 kilogram) specimen in California swallowed a piece of metal early in 1978, vets took immense pains to relieve the animal of its discomfort. They ruled out using forceps as potentially damaging to the dolphin's internal organs. Instead, they rolled up their sleeves and tried, one by one, to reach the offending article with their own hands. Unfortunately, strain as they might down the dolphin's throat, the metal remained out of reach.

The dolphin was in great pain. The vets at the hospital pondered the problem anxiously. Then they came up with a flash of inspiration. They procured the services of Clifford Ray, a professional basketball player with California's Golden State Warriors. Like many leading practitioners of the sport, Ray had exceptionally long arms—3 feet 9 inches (114 centimeters) to be precise. Ray reached deep into the dolphin's mouth—and succeeded where the vets failed. The metal was retrieved from deep the creature and a dolphin's life was saved.

Speaking of animals ingesting things they shouldn't, dogs will eat themselves into oblivion if allowed. They will even eat things that no other creature would likely ever think of as food.

The Magic of Snails

In March 1846, a collection of snail shells from Egypt and Greece was presented to the British Museum. Two of the Egyptian shells were gummed down on a plaque in a display cabinet.

Four years later, in March 1850, a glassy secretion was noticed around the mouth of one of the shells. The specimen was removed and placed in tepid water. After some ten minutes, a snail emerged and began to tour the rim of the basin.

Five months later it was still alive, and, according to the *Annals and Magazine of Natural History*, it "feeds readily, preferring cabbage-leaf to lettuce or any other kind of food yet tried."

Talk about taking a long nap!

A case that comes to mind is that of a three-year-old Great Dane who fell ill in 2014. When his concerned owners took him to the veterinarian they discovered the pooch had devoured forty-three socks!

The animal had to undergo emergency surgery to save its life.

Animals at Work

Mankind has always seemed very eager to put animals to work. These "beasts of burden" help plow our fields, provide transportation, and turn millwheels among countless other duties. One invention however, caused considerable outcry during the 1870s. This was the dog-driven sewing machine. The apparatus was marketed and actually used in some English households, employing a special set of wheels that were moved by a little dog on a leash. The dog trotted around a movable disc in a never-ending circle, providing power to the sewing machine. The people, however, were becoming sensitive to the mistreatment of animals during this time period, and the curious apparatus was banned after pressure from the Society for the Prevention of Cruelty to Animals.

Of course things can also go a bit too far in the other direction. An engineer from California named Mathewson, who was also a passionate lover of horses, was worried that the smoke and noise from the new steam trams—which were like trolley cars—were alarming the city's horses that pulled little cabs around town. To calm their fears Mathewson devised a special steam tram designed to look like a horse, with a gigantic horse's head mounted on the front. The bizarre vehicle traveled the streets of San Francisco for some time, but the commercial failure of the venture bankrupted the unfortunate inventor. I'm sure it was very calming to the city's horses to see this gigantic mechanical horse bearing down on them.

Animals have been harnessed to the needs of humanity in a variety of ingenious ways. In December 1970, for example, it was reported that the United States Navy was testing three particularly intelligent and alert dolphins as submarine trackers to monitor enemy underwater activity in South Vietnam. An interesting sidelight on the report was offered by the *Times* of that month, which described how the story, carried by Reuters press agency, was originally filed in French. Startled news editors first read that "three black infantry soldiers of particular intelligence and sensitive ear" were to be used in the underwater tests. There followed a correction about the test subjects: "three black guinea pigs of particular intelligence and sensitive ear." Finally, Reuters got it right, and issued a note of explanation: "The original French-language text uses the word *Marsouin*. According to the dictionary, this translates as 'dolphin,' 'colonial infantry man,' and 'guinea pig.' Regrettably, we came up with the right translation on the third try only."

The use of animals in warfare is not new. It was revealed in 1970 for example, that the Germans had tried to destroy Britain's potato crops with beetle bombs. The bombs consisted of containers filled with Colorado beetles, and the first was dropped on the Isle of Wight in 1943; evacuee children helped to round up the beetles. And of course who can forget the plot gone awry of using velociraptors as super soldiers in 2015's blockbuster film *Jurassic World*. Yeah, I know that's fiction, but is it that far off the track?

The terrifying reputation of certain creatures has also been harnessed to the needs of law enforcement. In 1981, for example, two red-kneed tarantulas from South America did service as security guards at a jewelry exhibition in the Bede Gallery at Jarrow.

The gallery owner found he could hire tarantulas from a pet shop for just a few dollars a month, plus a daily supply of maggot-like mealworms—an enticing charge compared with having to pay for human guards at an earlier exhibition. For six weeks, the spiders were encased with the jewelry as a deterrent to would-be thieves. "Crooks hate things like dogs and spiders," explained the owner. The pet shop proprietor dismissed the dangers. Tarantulas get to know the hand that feeds them and wouldn't sting unless provoked by sudden movement. The sting itself is rarely worse than that of a bee. Tarantulas are really very friendly; the pet shop had sold four as Christmas presents.

Using animals as protection can also go a bit too far. In August 1981, a Philadelphia man who carried a python in a bag as protection against muggers was arrested for recklessly endangering another person. The person in question was a policeman. The snake bit the policeman, who clubbed it to death with his truncheon.

The *Observer* of August 1982 announced a less alarming development in animal crime-busting. Prison drug rackets in Canada are to be tackled by a team of highly trained gerbils. Selected for their keen sense of smell and trained at a secret government location, these small mouselike creatures are to revolutionize the fight against the smuggling of drugs into federal penitentiaries.

The gerbils' potential was developed by the Correctional Services of Canada, a body responsible for the nation's main prisons. Gerbils have already proved their worth in sniffing out drug smugglers at airports. They have various advantages over tracker dogs, needing little food or space, being relatively quiet, and loyal to more than one handler. The special gerbils are kept at prison gates, trained not only to sniff out various drugs but to press alarm bells if they smell narcotics.

While we have traditionally come to expect the use of dogs in security and protection, there have been other types of animals utilized in recent years. In Melbourne, Florida,

Would this tarantula serve as an effective security guard? A gallery owner let two spiders mingle with exhibited jewels to deter theft.

there is a religious compound that employs peacocks to sound their very loud alert whenever someone ventures onto the property. Ironically, these birds are believed to be the direct descendants of peacocks once used by a drug dealer in Melbourne in the early 1980s.

Geese and swans, known to be aggressive and territorial, have also been used as security forces. And llamas, believe it or not, make perfect protectors of sheep and other livestock when there is a threat of attack from wolves or coyotes.

All monkeys are clever, but some are cleverer than others. A particular prodigy was Johnnie, a rhesus monkey owned by an Australian farmer. The monkey could drive a tractor and turn left or right on command.

Lost Property

Animals, much to our wonder, turn up in the strangest places. In 1929, a passenger on Imperial Airways left behind a tortoise wrapped in pink cotton wool. The back of the animal's shell was studded with rubies, emeralds, and other stones.

A lost alligator was once found on the Southern Railway, and a porpoise was discovered propped up in one of the cubicles of a men's lavatory in Scotland. The sixty-four-pound carcass was identified as a porpoise by a museum curator. Nobody knew how it had come into the lavatory. One gentleman told the *Times*: "We had heavy rain and there was flooding, but this is ridiculous."

In the Florida town of Indian Harbour Beach in 2014, a shark was discovered swimming around in the landlocked freshwater pond of Gleason Park. Town officials hired a shark fisherman to catch the eating machine before all the park's turtles and beautiful aquatic birds vanished.

No one is really sure how the shark wound up there. One theory is that it was caught in the ocean and deposited there as a prank. The other is that it may have been dropped by an Osprey who couldn't quite handle the shark and then simply adapted and grew in the pond.

One report shared a deeply disquieting experience when an unsuspecting man opened a beer and the head of a 16-inch (40 cm) snake popped out. Happily, the snake was dead, but how it had got into the bottle remained a mystery.

Sometimes, of course, the discovery of an animal in an unusual setting is the result of a deliberate escape bid. "Ape pole-vaults over park moat," announced the *Times* on July 18, 1978. The head keeper at Longleat Safari Park, Wiltshire, England, had been badly mauled by a chimpanzee which escaped from an island by polevaulting across a park using an 8-foot (2 meter) pole. The head keeper recovered from his wounds; and the recaptured chimp was put down.

Sad too, was the fate of Bubbles, another freedom-hungry zoo inmate, whose escapade kept Californians enthralled for nearly three weeks in the spring of 1978. During the early months of that year, the weather provided an apocalyptic setting for Bubbles's adventure. After weeks of torrential rain, the hills and cliffs of California had dissolved into swamps of mud and boulder, blocking main roads for miles. That's when it was reported that Bubbles, a 4,000-pound (1,814 kg) hippopotamus was strolling down a main thoroughfare in Orange County, with almost the whole California Highway Patrol on her tail and the traffic piled up behind her.

Bubbles was an inmate of the Lion Country Safari Animal Park and had normally been happy enough to remain on the lake where her keepers confined her. Perhaps it was the drama

When an animal escapes from a zoo or wildlife refuge, it can wreak havoc on the streets, as in the case of Bubbles the hippopotamus.

of the deluge that had quickened her sense of adventure. Anyway, Bubbles escaped from the safari park and found herself another lake; unfortunately, it bordered a much-used highway where the hippo posed a weighty problem for motorists.

For days, police and park rangers stalked her with tranquillizer guns, and on several occasions managed to hit her with doped darts. Bubbles remained fully conscious and entirely unconcerned. Then, after some twenty days on the loose, Bubbles unaccountably keeled over and died. The cause of death was not apparent and a postmortem was carried out on the body. It is thought that she was hit by two tranquillizer darts more or less simultaneously, with consequences that could not have been foreseen. In all events, the great Californian hippo hunt was over.

These Animals Are Dangerous

With one YouTube animal video going viral after another, it's easy for many of us to "humanize" all animals and think of them as tame and funny creatures that provide hours of amusing video hijinks. But, of course, the truth is that many are wild and very dangerous animals.

But nature is red in tooth and claw, and practically any creature may turn nasty. Reports of savage assaults flood in almost daily from around the world.

Australian train driver Danny Pocock learned a thing or two about the power of kangaroos in 1982 while walking to work.

A red kangaroo seemed to spring from nowhere and felled him with a series of expert punches. Mr. Pocock described his ordeal as "terrifying, he went up like a boxer and hit me with an almighty thump. He knocked me down three times altogether ... and I lost all three rounds."

That same year in Germany a twenty-year-old woman got a powerful response when she patted a horse. The horse sank its teeth into her and wouldn't let go even when bystanders hit it with sticks. The woman finally freed herself by biting the animal on its nostrils.

As referenced briefly a little earlier, man biting animal is news. The Nepali rice farmer mentioned earlier was minding his own business in 2012 when he felt a sharp pain in the very early hours. It was still dark outside. He looked down and saw that a snake had bitten him.

The man, Mohammed Salmodin, said that when he realized a snake had bitten him, he ran home to get a flashlight to see what kind of snake it was. When he saw that it was a poisonous cobra, Salmodin grabbed the slithery reptile and bit it over and over again until it died.

He later explained to reporters that he had taken the advice of a snake charmer he had spoken to once. "A snake charmer told me that if a snake bites you, bite it until it is dead and nothing will happen to you," he said.

Maybe there was something to the snake charmer's advice. Salmodin went back to work and only went to the hospital at the urging of his family later after he was done for the day. He was perfectly fine.

The following headlines help tell the story that animals are, well, unpredictable to say the least.

"Three Handicapped Monkeys Mug Mountain Men": In China, police were scouring the slopes of one of the country's holiest mountains for three mugger monkeys who, according to newspapers, had been robbing tourists and pilgrims. "Each of the three old monkeys has a physical defect. One is harelipped, another is one-eyed and the third has only three fingers on its right hand," the paper said. It appeared that the terrible trio had been attacking visitors to Omei mountain in the central district of China and stealing watches and bags. Tourists were advised to bring food as a bribe to distract the monkeys' attention, making escape possible.

The mugger monkey headline vies for startling effect with the classic simplicity of the following item, which appeared in a London newspaper in 1948:

> *"Hare Shoots Man—And escapes from car window" Johannesburg, Tuesday. A motorist from East London shot a hare and threw it into the back seat of his car. The hare was only stunned and, regaining consciousness, touched off the trigger of the gun as it leapt out of the window. The shot wounded the motorist in the neck.*

"Woman Savaged by a Dead Sheep!": So far as I know, this headline has never appeared in a major newspaper. The incident was, however, the subject of a humorous note in 1982 in the *Times Diary*. While food writer Philippa Davenport was preparing for her demonstration in Harrod's new cookshop, a frozen leg of lamb fell from the top of her freezer and laid her out. Ms. Davenport was badly concussed, and taken to hospital.

While solo assaults by maverick animals, dead or alive, have been the cause of alarm, how much more terrible are mass attacks? Plagues of snakes or spiders are commonly reported in Australia, South Africa, India, South America, and elsewhere. During an exceptionally hot spell in July 1975, for example, more than two hundred snakes were taken out of a swimming pool at an empty mansion in Purley, Surrey. The snakes had apparently slithered in to escape the heat. More unlikely still was the great invasion of August 1982, which took place in the outskirts of London:

"Hamster Horror—Superhamster Feared" screamed the headlines. At Burnt Oak, hamsters were taking over. Some terrified residents had to be moved from their homes as these small, normally timorous creatures infested the council estate at Hook Walk. Hamster shields were set up to protect houses, especially around television aerial lines which the animals used as routes up walls and into bedrooms. One resident, with his son, aged fifteen, told reporters that they had trapped and killed nearly two hundred. The council was besieged with complaints.

Hamsters were first introduced into Britain as pets in the 1930s; it was thought that those of Burnt Oak were descended from the normal species but had somehow escaped captivity and gone wild, thriving in Dumpsters and trash heaps, adapting to the harsh English winter. The Ministry of Agriculture was consulted and a number of poisons tried—all without success. Experts feared that the hamsters' ability to resist both poisons and cold weather showed that they were on their way to becoming superhamsters. Unchecked, they could spread over the rest of the country, disturbing the food chain and posing serious problems for agriculture.

Barnet council ordered an all-out offensive. Officials came in rubber boots, armed to the teeth with traps and bait. But the hamsters were too quick for them. Not one of the furry pests was caught after the campaign began. Zoologists blamed the council's methods; tractor mowers had been used to clear overgrown gardens, driving the hamsters underground. One expert, quoted in the *Hendon Times* said: "Barnet council really don't know much about the habits of hamsters at all—hamsters burrow several feet down."

Perhaps the hamsters had moved on to improve their stock elsewhere. Or perhaps they still lurk in secret burrows beneath Burnt Oak, waiting, waiting ...

In southern US states like Georgia, North Carolina, and Florida, the vulture migration can get a little ugly and a little scary. It seems that when vultures find a place to roost and call home, they are very difficult to scare off. The carrion-eating birds normally head south for the winter in search of food. Since they are a federally protected species, they cannot be harmed or hunted.

One beautiful home in Brevard County, Florida, had such a problem in 2008. Vultures started camping out on the pool room, on the screened-in pool enclosure, and on the front lawn. Never mind the fact that they ripped holes throughout the entire pool enclosure, but they also defecated all over the place causing a stink to go along with the unsightly appearance.

All types of experts were brought in to try and remove the birds. Nothing seemed to work. They even tried fireworks, and that only seemed to rile the birds up more. Finally, one expert hung a dead vulture on a long stick attached to the house.

That did the trick. They started flying away and moved out of the neighborhood.

I guess seeing one of their own in that state was just too much to handle. Actually, according to experts, they do not like seeing other vultures in "unnatural" positions.

In 2013, the town of Bridgewater, New Jersey, called in an expert who hung dead vultures from trees all over town to drive away a flock that had settled in the town.

America's Urban Alligators

One of the most recurrent pieces of newspaper lore about New York life is the story that the city's sewer system is inhabited by hordes of prowling alligators. The alligators, so the tales go, are the onetime pets of eccentric New Yorkers who, having grown tired of them, flush them into the sewer system. Anyone who has ever lived in New York has heard the stories.

The chief of the city's underground drainage and aqueduct system is constantly pestered with inquiries about the awesome, subterranean prowlers. Time and again he has refuted the tales. There are no alligators in New York sewers. No authenticated case of an alligator encounter has ever been reported. New York's alligators are fiction, not fact.

Then, in August 1982, the drainage department was confounded. An alligator was caught in the water system. Measuring only 26 inches (66 cm) long, she was hardly the nightmare creature of press legend; but an alligator she was, "large as life and twice as snappy," according to one report. She was snared in a reservoir which supplies the city's drinking water about 25 miles (40 km) north of Manhattan. An expert told reporters: "The way to catch the things is to wait until dark and then shine a light in their eyes."

This handy tip for catching alligators has greater value in America's southern states, where the razor-toothed reptiles are a more menacing presence. Alligators are native to the southern deltas, but until recent years they had practically been exterminated by hunters who obtained high prices for their skins. Then, in the late 1960s, alligators became a protected species and began to make their comeback with a vengeance. A particularly nasty infestation occurred at Homosassa Springs, Florida, in 1966 and was the subject of much attention in the national press.

By the late 1970s, alligators were becoming a fairly common sight in Miami and other southern cities. They turned up in people's backyards and swimming pools. Once in a while, an alligator would snap up a poodle or other pet. In the summer of 1977, motorists in downtown Miami could hardly believe their eyes. For there, sprawled on a sidewalk at a major road junction, were two quite colossal alligators, apparently waiting for the traffic lights to change.

Cars screeched to a halt amid a riot of horn honking. The police were summoned as terrified pedestrians raced from the scene. But by the time the police arrived, the alligators had slunk off to the nearest sewer.

Of course, being cold-blooded creatures, they would never be able to survive long in the sewers, as they need sunlight to survive.

In 2015, an alligator helped law enforcement catch a burglar on the run...with deadly results. Police had caught up with twenty-two-year-old burglary suspect Matthew Riggins in Barefoot Bay, Florida – a large retirement community. Instead of giving up peacefully, Riggins fled and decided to hide in a nearby lake. Well, the saying in Florida is that every single body of water has at least one alligator in it and this one was no exception. Unfortunately for Riggins, he never made it out of the water.

Police reported hearing Riggins screaming but could not tell where it was coming from because it was dark. In the morning they found his body near an 11-foot (3.3-meter) gator, who did not want to part with his prize easily.

The medical examiner listed the cause of death as alligator attack.

Late Lamented Pets

On July 13, 1982, a teacher fired his starting pistol to demonstrate what pupils should expect on sports day, and the class's pet hamster died of a heart attack.

In 1978, animal lovers jammed the switchboards at a television station to complain about a news item concerning a cat. The item was about an emergency call from an old lady, whose cat was stuck up in a tree. The incident occurred during a firemen's strike of January that year, and so army soldiers responded to the call. They rescued the old woman's cat from the tree and she invited them in for tea. They accepted gratefully, then left. Unfortunately, they ran over the rescued cat on their way back to the barracks.

CHAPTER TWO: DISORDERLY CONDUCT

PERFECTLY NORMAL PEOPLE

"The Night the Human Birdman Gatecrashed on the Bard" was how one newspaper's headline recounted an incident that occurred during an open-air Shakespeare in the Park performance. While the play was in progress, a man dressed as a chicken forced his way onto the stage and disrupted the production. The show was stopped and the man was ushered from the stage. He was eventually found by police, smelling strongly of alcohol and standing in a pond.

While the case was being heard in court, people on the public benches began to laugh. They were sternly rebuked by the magistrate, who told them, "This is no laughing matter." Now there is a judge in need of a sense of humor.

Clothing, costumes, or the lack of either has resulted in more than one juicy story. In England in 1981 a company fired an employee who came to work wearing a succession of eccentric and undignified hats. The man fought for his job and the case was brought before an industrial tribunal, which heard that the man had been fired after he arrived wearing a hat with a replica of Kermit the Frog on top. The tribunal ruled that under the circumstances, wearing a Kermit hat was not a good reason for dismissal. I wonder what he wore to work the following day?

In Colorado in 2014, a group known as "Free the Nipple" sued the city of Fort Collins for criminalizing women who expose their nipples in public but not men. Ironically, the city of

Boulder—only a forty-five-minute drive away—welcomed female toplessness and is a favorite destination among nudists. The group's stated goal is gender equality. So far, thirty states have relaxed laws regarding topless women.

One thing about the human race is that we sometimes tend to hold onto a grudge, sometimes for the silliest reasons. The feud between college professors Alan Sandage and Halton Arp was waged in an inconspicuous, but no less bitter fashion. It was learned in 1977 that for ten years the two men had occupied offices in the same corridor of the California Institute of Technology. In all that time they refused to exchange a single word. The cause of contention? They disagreed about the distance from the earth of certain objects in the universe.

Yep, we hold onto things for a long time. Just ask private eye David Lewis, whose obsession with a crossword puzzle is

A man dressed as a chicken was arrested for disrupting a production of Shakespeare in the Park.

the definition of perseverance. On April 23, 1933, he sat down with that week's crossword puzzle. In August of 1982, he finally sent in his solution—almost fifty years after he had first embarked on it. "Sorry I'm late, the clues rather baffled me," he wrote, adding: "By the time I finished the crossword I could hardly recognize the handwriting I had when I started."

Despite his decades-long marathon effort, the sixty-seven-year-old Cardiff, England, man still got a few of the answers wrong.

In Brevard County, Florida, a judge who had gotten fed up with a public defender's stalling tactics challenged the attorney to a fistfight in the hallway. After the scuffle, the judge returned to the courtroom to a cheering gallery.

However, the Florida Supreme Court ordered Judge John C. Murphy to retire. He not only embarrassed himself and disgraced the judiciary, they ruled, but when he returned to the courtroom, he proceeded to handle half a dozen cases with-

THE WORLD'S WEIRDEST WAR

In June 1969, the Central American football teams of Honduras and El Salvador played a series of qualifying matches for the World Cup. The games were closely fought, and El Salvador eventually won after being awarded a disputed penalty. Rioting broke out at the grounds, and the fighting spilled into the streets. In July, war was declared between the two countries as a direct result of the disputed penalty. Two thousand people died in the fighting. In the next round of the World Cup, the El Salvador team was eliminated.

out the public defender present—a clear violation. The case made the rounds in monologues of late night television hosts.

In Philadelphia, a man who had stolen a chewing-gum vending machine containing 250 pieces was once sentenced by a judge to chew every tab of gum in the machine. He was required to drop a penny in the slot for every piece taken out. The task completed, he had to go and give the machine, with the pennies in it, back to its owner.

A more worthwhile activity was devised by a Miami judge in June 1982. Learning that the South Florida blood service was in constant need of donors, he gave minor offenders the choice of either paying a fine or giving a pint of their own blood.

Another judge ordered one couple who had skipped out on jury duty to donate $500 of food to the local soup kitchen or risk going to jail.

Love, Marriage, and Family Life

In 1981, a New Jersey man was indicted for biting the nose off his daughter's boyfriend. Not long afterward, a fifteen-year-old girl in Italy was admitted to the hospital seeking treatment for a dislocated jaw; she told doctors that the injury was caused by passionate kisses (her boyfriend was unhurt).

The perils of passion were illustrated in August 1982, when doctors warned that love bites that break on the skin can be fatal; only bites from rabid animals were more serious. New York doctors reported hospitals overflowing with patients bitten on ears, noses, hands, nipples, and genitals. In some cases, infections had led to septic shock and death. Special dangers were reported from injuries that did not even look like bites "because some people have incomplete dentures."

In 2016, the Eastern European state of Georgia issued a census in order to count and understand the "single" people in the country. The fear was that not enough people were getting married and repopulating the country. The questions on the census included the usual things like height, weight, and age but also asked what the person's Zodiac sign was!

What, after all, is love? In September 1977, psychologists and others met in England for the first-ever conference on the subject that has mystified poets since the dawn of time. Their conclusion? Love is "the cognitive-affective state characterized by intrusive or obsessive fantasizing concerning reciprocity of amorant feelings by the object of the amorance." Ah, so that explains it.

Love and the pain that sometimes accompanies it are not unique to the human world. In June 2016, a killer whale, possibly still heartbroken from being captured and separated from its loved ones, leapt from its tank in the Canary islands and refused to go back in the water. Newspapers described the whale as suicidal and heartbroken.

Family love can sometimes get ugly as well. In 2016, a father in Texas was arrested after he challenged his daughter to a firearm duel. Yep, that's right. Walk ten paces, turn and fire. According to police, Robert Williams had been arguing with his daughter when he pulled a gun on her. He then ordered her to go to another room and fetch a gun so they could duel.

The age of the daughter was not released but police said they each fired their weapon once before Williams grabbed a shotgun and threatened his wife. The wife and daughter managed to escape the home and Williams was arrested.

"Bride's Mother Kills Groom at Reception" was an unfortunate headline in the 1980s from Colorado. The groom was indeed shot dead with a rifle bullet during a terrible fight that erupted only six hours after the wedding ceremony. But the headline was slightly misleading. The mother-in-law hit the groom by accident; she was really aiming at her husband.

A more mellow mother-in-law report was issued from Colorado in the same summer, concerning the marriage of John and Paula Morris. Paula was a highly successful announcer with a local radio station. She had married John on the understanding that they should not start a family until her career was entirely secure. So when their unplanned baby son, Jason, was born only a year later, Paula grew concerned about her future.

To solve the problem, John Morris gave up his job as a ski instructor and agreed to look after the child. If he needed any assistance, Paula's widowed mother, Paulette Jamieson, who lived nearby, was at hand.

The arrangement worked well enough for two years, but collapsed one evening in 1982 when Paula arrived home after a long stint at the radio station and John informed her: "I'm suing for divorce." He added: "You have become a disinterested mother and wife because of your career. Your mother and I are in love. We want to marry and also take custody of little Jason."

Paula moved out of the house that night, and soon afterwards countersued for divorce, accusing her mother of adultery and also bringing a case against her mother for alienation of affection. Forty-four-year-old Mrs. Jamieson, a striking blonde, told reporters: "I don't suppose my daughter will speak to me ever again. I'm deeply sorry about that. But she has her career to think of. I have little Jason to consider."

The divorce case was one of the most complex heard in Colorado. In contrast, a very rapid conclusion was reached in Jacksonville, Florida, in December 1972. Rudell Hickson and his wife, Mary, were in a divorce court trying to be separated. Instead, they got into an argument, both pulled guns, and blazed away at each other from opposite ends of a conference table in the judge's hearing room. Bullets flew in all directions.

A police officer was giving testimony in an adjoining courtroom when the gun battle broke out. He borrowed a pistol from a circuit judge, chased Mrs. Hickson down the hall and ordered her to halt. When she failed to do so, he shot the unfortunate woman dead.

Sometimes, of course, one partner in a marriage may refuse to grant the divorce desired by the other. Many and various are the solutions to which frustrated individuals have resorted. Thomas Karkanias, for example, a bus conductor from central Greece, was charged with rigging up the stove exhaust vent to murder his wife by electrocution. A South African woman in Johannesburg's wealthy white suburbs was charged with trying to poison her husband by treating his hamburger with swimming pool chemicals.

However, not all divorce stories end this poorly or even in real divorce. Stephen and Deborah Ehrhardt were done. They were ready to move on from their thirty-year marriage and call it quits. The economy had tanked, and by 2014 so, it seemed, had their love. They went down to the Florida courthouse to sign the final papers.

Judge A. B. Majeed sensed something. He told the couple to reconsider. He noted how they were still friendly and there appeared to be no bitterness. Maybe he noticed one still-flickering ember of love. In any event, the judge's words struck a chord, but the couple signed the divorce papers anyway.

They walked out of the courthouse together and, it being lunchtime, decided to go for lunch at a nearby Chili's restaurant. They got along so well that Deborah invited him back to the house to watch movies that same night.

Stephen never left.

In 2015, a year later, the couple remarried and made sure to thank the judge for whatever words he used that stuck with them.

In general, however, jealous love must surely be the most common motive for crimes of violence. The love triangle has provided the theme for countless works of pulp fiction, as well as for some of the world's greatest works of literature.

These lovelorn torments were experienced by Englishman Graham Street.

According to the *Daily Telegraph* newspaper in 1974, Street literally flew into action on a homemade catapult when he saw his wife with another man. He made a springboard out of a long plank and two car tires, and after a long run-up launched himself into the air. Propelled at high speed, Street crashed head-first through the kitchen window of the house where his wife was embracing the other man. The human cannonball landed in the sink and slid gently to the floor.

Street plead guilty to breaking the window and was told by the judge not to indulge in such "amateur dramatics" again.

Clearly Street's motive was jealousy. But what caused a woman named Linda Hughes to stab her husband fifteen times with a kitchen knife as he lay peacefully sleeping in 1978? Not even she could provide a satisfactory answer; she was as bewildered by her actions as everyone else.

Hughes was brought for trial accused of wounding her husband Frank with intent to cause grievous bodily harm. The court heard how her husband was taken to the hospital with collapsed lungs after his wife's savage assault. But Hughes herself was asleep at the time. She was freed when the prosecution dropped the charges, admitting that: "According to psychiatric opinion it is certainly feasible that what she did, she did in her sleep." The judge agreed that no purpose would be served by a trial.

"I just cannot explain what happened," the woman told reporters. "Apparently I am what is called a disturbed sleeper. But there is no other reason for it. I was half asleep when I got up to peel some potatoes for the next day. I must have had the knife from then." The couple had been happily married for ten years and had two children. The moaning husband managed to awaken his spouse during the course of the attack. She said, "You can imagine what an awful shock it was when I saw what was happening. I telephoned for an ambulance straight away."

The happy couple left the court arm-in-arm.

Curious Crime

In 2016, the Croatian soccer club Zagreb reported that someone had broken into their training facility and made off with the team's tractor. The machine was specially tuned to mow the grass for that particular soccer field.

Japanese investigators are still puzzled by the ongoing theft of subway passenger straps, you know, the straps that people hold onto when there aren't any seats for them. Between 2015 and early 2016 nearly two hundred of the straps went missing from Japanese passenger trains, including eleven in one day from a single passenger car. The bizarre thefts have given the

The $20,000 handshake? A banker was sued for shaking a woman's hand too vigorously in church.

normally very ordered Japanese society a jolt. Newspaper accounts describe the thefts as ghastly and creepy.

The Trouser Thief of Toronto was apprehended in 1938. For thirty-three years he had stolen nothing but trousers. "His record goes back to 1905," said the prosecutor, "and only once, in 1907, did he lapse from his standard and steal anything but a pair of trousers. On that occasion it was a shirt."

It's clear that people will try just about anything. One man believed he would be free from suspicion because of his physical condition. But when he stepped off a plane from Caracas, Venezuela, he was arrested by narcotics agents in New York.

The agents came up empty-handed when they searched his luggage. Then, noticing his wooden leg, they took him to the nearest hospital and removed it in the presence of a doctor. Hidden in a compartment in the leg, neatly encased in a plastic bag, was 8 ounces (226 grams) of cocaine, worth $65,000.

The man pleaded guilty to drug possession and was sentenced to four years in prison. While serving his term, the smuggler made an appeal against the validity of the search, claiming that federal agents had violated his right to privacy. The appeal was launched with a cheerful optimism and it was turned down.

A forty-five-year-old Dusseldorf man lodged no such appeal, but then his plan had been twice as ambitious. In 1978, in Bangkok, he was jailed for five years for trying to smuggle about 2 pounds (.9 kg) of morphine out of Thailand in his two artificial legs.

It's probably safe to say that New York's JFK Airport has seen it all when it comes to arrivals trying to smuggle drugs into the country. In 2014, airport officials released a report and photographs of some of the most imaginative or bizarre attempts at drug smuggling. One woman was arrested after her attempt at hiding a skull-shaped packet of cocaine beneath her wig. A British couple was arrested after sewing packets of drugs under their pet dog's skin.

Other attempts include salt and pepper shakers filled with drugs, books with drugs laced into the pages, and even frozen meat filled with drugs. Of course there is also the woman who literally had too much junk in the trunk and was arrested after inspectors found that her fake booty was actually made of cocaine.

The action, or rather handshake, of a Philadelphia banker might have been considered a crime by at least one couple. The man shook hands with a Philadelphia woman after church service. Two years later, the woman claimed, her hand still hurt and she brought a suit against the banker for $10,000 in damages. Her husband launched a related suit on his own behalf. Seeking $10,000 for himself because he had been "deprived of his wife's assistance in society"; the case of the Golden Handshake.

The banker was accused of negligence in "pulling, squeezing, and shaking the woman's hand" without considering the strength and power of his hand grip.

The case of two senior citizens of Cleveland, Ohio, provides a tale of the World's Worst Gunslingers. After the event, which occurred in 1981, they were released having signed papers saying that they did not wish to press charges against one another and their names were not released. One, however, was aged seventy-seven and the other seventy-six.

The men had a grudge that went back a long way. They lived opposite one another and began quarrelling in the narrow hallway of an apartment house one Tuesday morning. On this occasion, however, mere insults could not quench their rage. Each went back to his apartment block and returned brandishing a venerable six-shooter.

Both shot their full load—twelve bullets were fired in all—and alarmed residents called the police. "There were bullet holes above, bullet holes down, and bullet holes all over the hallway," said a detective. But every one had gone astray. The gunslingers missed because one needed a cane to prop himself up and the other had trouble seeing because of glaucoma. They were standing just 5 feet (1.5 m) apart during the duel.

Domestic Lock-Ups

Much like a children's rhyme about getting stuck in the restroom, fact almost imitated fiction in August 1982, when two elderly French ladies suffered a long period of incarceration. A widow of ninety-four and her sixty-six-year-old daughter spent nine days locked in a bathroom at their Paris apartment. They had been forced inside the room by a burglar who jammed two armchairs against the door before fleeing. Their cries were not heard, and they survived on water from the sink until a worried relative contacted the police.

In China in 2016, rescue workers came to the aid of a man who had gotten stuck inside the washing machine he was trying to repair. It took them about an hour to free him, and the toughest part was making sure the man had enough oxygen to breathe while they worked carefully to remove the drum from the machine.

In recent years, Chinese firefighters rescued a woman who had gotten stuck between two walls while searching for something she had dropped and a little boy whose head had gotten stuck in his father's car's sunroof.

Panic in the Streets

In March 1957, villagers in England noted a sinister, glowing object hovering ominously over their small community. From it emanated an eerie white light. So great was local concern about the UFO that questions were even asked in Parliament about it. Were the aliens poised for invasion?

The answer came in the House of Commons, when the Air Minister was questioned about the UFO sighting. Amid laughter, an under-secretary replied: "This object, which was described in the Press as a flying saucer, did not emanate from outer space, but from a laundry. It consisted of two hydrogen-filled balloons illuminated by a flashlight bulb and devised by a laundry mechanic."

Questioned by reporters, the mechanic revealed himself to be an amateur meteorologist who had created the device as an experiment in tracing air currents.

The case is just one among many UFO flaps. On New Year's Eve in 1978, for example, television viewers throughout Europe were riveted by the screening of some mysterious objects filmed over New Zealand. At the same time, a cigar-shaped craft with flaming portholes was widely reported in Europe itself. A surgeon and his neighbor, a builder, were among the first to spot the object. "It was cigar-shaped with a broad, trailing vapor jet," said the surgeon. "It moved in a straight line with no noise. I have always been skeptical about these things, but this defied any orthodox analysis." His neighbor confirmed the description: he saw "portholes aflame with incandescence."

Though some controversy still lingers around the New Zealand sightings, the cigar-shaped craft proved easier to explain. It was the burning debris of a Soviet rocket, which had launched a satellite into space and crashed in Germany.

UFO flaps have generally resulted from honest mistakes and have seldom caused long-term distress. A very different kind of panic gripped the small French village of Pont-Saint-Esprit in August 1951. It was as if a collective hysteria of medieval intensity had struck the community. Contemporary English language newspapers dealt only briefly with the story, but a full account is given in *The Day of St. Anthony's Fire* by John G. Fuller (Hutchinson, 1969).

Hundreds of inhabitants felt the symptoms: giddiness, diarrhea, vomiting, and other effects. But for many the experience was much more alarming. Five-year-old Marie-Joseph Carle, for example, saw blood dripping from her bedroom ceiling; there were tigers by the wall and they were coming to eat her. Her father found himself endlessly counting the six panes on his window, day and night; flies were everywhere and he craved bead curtains for them to rest on. A young engineer could think of nothing but potatoes. Another man saw exploding flowers and knew the secrets of the universe.

It grew worse. Lying in his bedroom, M. Sauvet became a circus performer, a strong man whose pillow cases turned to iron bars, which he ripped to shreds effortlessly. Giant timbers splintered in his hands while an invisible audience of admirers cheered deliriously—his bedstead was ruined. The hallucinations were interspersed with bouts of exhausted lethargy when the unfortunate man knew who he was and lay in dread of the next convulsive fantasy.

The hospital was overflowing with victims of delusion, shrieking and moaning night after night. One man was being chased by bandits with huge donkey ears. Another was tormented by writhing red snakes in his brain. One woman spat fire from her fingers; another thought she was a baroness and deserved better treatment than she was getting.

There were only three straightjackets in the hospital, and though the place was ringed by police and firemen, moaning patients were constantly breaking loose and carrying their horrors back into the streets.

And the cause of this appalling visitation? A batch of loaves made by a village baker had been affected by ergot fungus, a mold which forms on certain grains and which causes psychic disturbance (LSD is an ergot alkaloid). Ergotism had been thought a thing of the past. In the Middle Ages, whole villages had sometimes been afflicted with a terrifying collective madness which was known as St. Anthony's fire; the episode at Pont-Saint-Esprit was a freak recurrence of the ancient malady. Five people died, and of the three hundred or so affected by the 'accursed bread' there were many who never truly recovered from their ordeal.

In 2009, the fear was not so much alien invaders when a UFO, or rather a runaway balloon, took over the nightly news. The worry was that six-year-old Falcon Heene had climbed inside his father's contraption that had gotten free from its constraints and was now on a high-speed free-for-all flight through Colorado.

Just about every news station cut into a live feed as the balloon reached heights of 7,000 feet (2,133 m)and travelled more than 50 miles (80 km) before finally coming to rest. When rescuers rushed to the balloon, they found it empty.

The family had lied, saying the boy was in the balloon when he was home the entire time. The publicity stunt was costly. The parents were charged and arrested, spent twenty or so days in jail, and were ordered to pay $36,000 in fines.

CHAPTER THREE: LONERS

THE CASE OF COLONEL BARKER

Early in 1927, Captain Leslie Ivor Victor Gauntlett Bligh Barker, a former cavalry officer, had a brush with the London police. Captain Barker was a prominent member of the fascist movement in London. Police had raided its headquarters, where the captain was found to be in possession of a pistol with a forged firearms certificate.

The case received little attention in the press. The captain was prosecuted at the Central Criminal Court for submitting a forged document with intention to deceive. Captain Barker made his way into the courtroom with his eyes bandaged. It was explained that the defendant suffered from bouts of blindness owing to wounds incurred during World War I. There was some sympathy for the ex-officer, with his distinguished service record. He was acquitted of the charge on the grounds that the certificate was not a public document.

Captain Barker was a popular figure who also ran a restaurant in the West End, and it was when this venture floundered, and Barker failed to appear in a bankruptcy court, that the sensational aspects of the story broke.

In March 1929, Colonel Barker, as he now styled himself; was arrested and taken to Brixton prison. When a routine medical examination was proposed, Colonel Barker objected. He could not submit to it, he said, because he was a woman.

Lillias Arkell-Smith passed herself off as Colonel Victor Barker in the 1920s, when transgendered individuals were less accepted by society.

The doctors examined the accused, and confirmed his story. The colonel was immediately taken to the women's prison at Holloway.

Who was he? How had he got away with his masquerade for so long? What were his motives? The press reports that followed were spangled with apostrophes referring to him and his exploits. This was considered shocking for the time.

When the astounding discovery was made, the newspapers scrambled for interviews with those who had known him. Old fascist movement members were nonplussed. Barker had hunted and boxed with them and seemed a jolly good fellow. *Evening Standard* reporters contacted J. Moss Ltd., a firm of military outfitters, whose bemused staff produced correspondence from the colonel recording their dealings with him. Only recently, Barker had come in for a new uniform, explaining that he had been promoted to staff colonel at the War Office: "He was always dressed well. His thick dark hair was always brushed well back from the forehead."

A former landlady said: "I think it was wonderful that he was able to keep up the pretense of a man. If I saw him again I should shake him by the hand."

But the most remarkable fact to emerge during the first interviews was that Colonel Barker had a wife and children.

The whole bizarre story unfolded over several weeks, first, as the press tracked down the wife, and later, as the colonel himself was prosecuted in court for obtaining a marriage license by deceit.

Colonel Barker's maiden name was Lillias Irma Valerie Barker. Legally, she was Mrs. Arkell-Smith. The daughter of a William Barker, she was born on August 26, 1895. In 1912 she was sent to a convent in Brussels, and when war broke out she served as a nurse in a Surrey hospital. Later she was employed at an army remount depot.

Later she married Lieutenant Harold Arkell-Smith, an Australian. It was only six months, however, before they separated. After the war she helped to run a tea shop and while there she met another Australian soldier named Pearce-Crouch. Her life of deception began with a modest masquerade. The couple started living together as man and wife, and by Pearce-Crouch she bore two children, a boy and a girl.

But Pearce-Crouch was a violent man, and the relationship appears to have been stormy. While passing as the Australian's wife, Barker took to wearing men's clothing. And dressed in this fashion, she started to develop a liaison with Alfreda Haward, the daughter of a local chemist.

She told the girl that she was really a man, and her name was Sir Victor Barker, a baronet. They began to go courting. Barker explained that his father was dead, and that his mother had forced him to wear women's clothing. Alfreda Haward apparently swallowed the story, and after a violent fight between Barker and Pearce-Crouch, the lovers eloped. On November 14, 1923, Sir Victor Barker and Miss Alfreda Haward were married at a Brighton church.

Was Miss Haward really deceived? By her own account she certainly was. It would be distasteful to speculate at length on what passed during the honeymoon. Barker told the girl that during the war he had received "serious abdominal wounds."

"I know it seems incredible that I could have been deceived as I was," Miss Haward told *Evening Standard* reporters, "but not once during the three years we lived together did I suspect that my husband was anything but what he pretended to be—a war injured officer." She did, however, doubt his claims to be a baronet: "I said it would be much better for both of us if he forgot the title. Frankly, I thought it was a little bit of conceit on his part, and assumed that he might have some distant claim to the title. Our life was fairly happy until towards the end of 1926, when I had to go into a nursing home to be operated on for appendicitis. After the operation I went down to Littlehampton to stay with my people until l recuperated. In January 1927 I received a letter from him saying that he had decided to finish with me and could not live with me again. It was a terrible blow to me, but I decided that I could do nothing but stay at home. I could not appeal to him. I was much too proud to do that.

"I know that some members of my own family were not keen on the marriage, particularly because my father could not find any reference to 'Sir Victor Barker' in our book of titles. I am afraid it was I who clinched matters by saying that I trusted Victor more than anybody in the world."

The discovery of Colonel Barker's masquerade came to her as a "thunderbolt"; she had first learned of it through the newspapers. During the *Evening Standard* interview, the girl's father said: "My daughter is a fine, straight girl, and it is dreadful to think that she has been deceived in this way. It has ruined her life. I thought she would be happy so I gave my consent to the marriage. I have since been blamed for not making more careful inquiries, and I wish to goodness now that I had." The girl's mother said: "It is terrible to think that a woman could be so wicked."

In a *Sunday Express* exclusive, Msiss Haward expanded on her marriage, presenting Colonel Barker as a near-ideal husband: "I always called him Bill," she said. "It is such a manly name. It suited him beautifully. I do not think we got on better or worse than countless couples. I think most people would say we were happy. Our marriage was a perfectly normal one." If her husband had a fault, it was his eye for the ladies. "Everything was all right until another woman came onto the scene. She made him do anything she wanted. He left me with scarcely an explanation. I always knew Bill was susceptible. He could never see a pretty woman without paying her compliments and saying pretty things to her.

"I must say 'he' and 'him' because anything else is strange to me. I cannot believe that he is anything else. It is too fantastic. I feel as if the whole thing is a fearful nightmare from which I shall wake up. I wish I could."

It was after leaving his wife that Barker got involved with the national fascist movement. And by a curious coincidence, the prosecutor at the trial over firearms possession was the same man who prosecuted Barker for giving a false name on his marriage license. The recorder at the later trial was astounded:

The recorder: "She stood trial in this court as a man?"

The prosecutor: "Yes. Not a soul in court—I prosecuted her on that occasion— was aware that there was other than a man in the dock."

Barker's defending counsel stated that there was no law against a woman dressing up as a man. He cited Joan of Arc, who had recently been canonized. Male clothing had been necessary to his client if she was to make a career for herself, having left Pearce-Crouch. Miss Haward's father was far from being reluctant to allow his daughter to marry the mystery baronet—it was he who had forced the couple into the ceremony. Barker did plead guilty, however, to the charge of knowingly and willfully causing a false statement to be entered on a register of marriage.

Lillias Arkell-Smith, alias "Colonel Barker," was found guilty and sentenced to nine months imprisonment. The case had exploded like a bombshell in an age where transgenderism was a subject less familiar to the general public than it is today. By any standards, however, it had been a bizarre affair, and some lenience was shown to the defendant on account of "what she had suffered owing to the great interest which the public has taken and is taking in her when she is going through the great ordeal of her life."

Fast-forward nearly a century and it is more than acceptable for someone like Olympic track and field champion Caitlyn Jenner to be recognized with numerous awards, magazine covers, and even a reality television series.

The Rational Dresser

An article in the *Penny Pictorial* magazine of January 20, 1900, billed her as "The Most Eccentric Woman in the World." It told readers: "Every adult in America who can read is able to answer the question, 'Who is Doctor Mary Walker?'" In England, it continued, readers were less likely to be familiar with the name, unless it evoked faint memories from some stray newspaper paragraph. For the English were then not much interested in the two questions of dress reform and higher education for women, issues that were then raging in the American press.

The women's rights pioneer Dr. Mary Walker was considered "weird" for wearing men's clothing.

Dr. Mary Walker, who died in 1919, was an important pioneer of women's rights. If contemporary newspapermen regarded her as the

World's Weirdest Woman, it was partly because her campaigns broke entirely new ground so far as the question of clothing was concerned. Dr. Walker regarded tight corseting and billowing skirts as unnecessary and unhygienic fetters of womanhood. "She has for the last forty years worn trousers," explained the awestruck article in the *Pictorial* magazine. Time and again she was arrested and imprisoned for wearing men's dress, though her record of service during the American Civil War ought to have earned her better treatment.

During the Civil War, she had been an assistant surgeon with the Union forces. She was wounded in battle and captured by the Confederates, who released her, however, when they discovered her true sex. Because of the injuries she received in the war, she sued the United States government for a pension. She was, nonetheless, the only woman to be awarded a bronze star for her wartime services. It might seem that the press dealt unfairly with what was, after all, a perfectly sensible campaign. Certainly, the good doctor looked rather strange in her top hat, frock coat, and cravat, but that was partly because of the absurdly fussy nature of contemporary male attire. Dr. Walker called it "rational dress"; by modern standards it was grotesquely irrational. Yet who today would complain of a woman in jeans and a T-shirt?

And yet, for all her common sense and humanity, it has to be admitted that Dr. Walker was something of an eccentric. For example, she founded a colony for women on a farm of 137 acres (55 ha) in upstate New York. It was occupied only by women, bound like nuns to celibacy—but unlike nuns the occupants had to wear men's clothing. She declared herself president of the community, which was governed by an annually elected management board. It had its own judges and policing system. Horses and bicycles were available for recreation, but there were no side saddles, as women rode during that time. All women were compelled to ride astride.

As for her personal vagaries, *Pictorial* magazine reported

a typical incident. She had recently walked into the shop of a well-known Washington photographer who immediately recognized her as the celebrated champion of rational dress.

"I want you to make a photograph of me in a coffin," said Dr. Walker. "Have you got a coffin handy in your studio? I want to see exactly how I shall look when I'm dead."

There was, as it happened, no coffin lying about the studio. Gamely, the photographer suggested that she might lie in a large crate in which a new iron bathtub had just arrived that was then lying in his back yard. He could cover it with curtains and muslin, he assured his customer, and no one would know the difference. So the crate was brought in, a sofa pillow was placed at the head, and Dr. Walker solemnly stepped in. Lying down, she closed her eyes and set her face as if in death.

The photographer carefully draped the crate with curtains, placed his camera in position, and prepared for the macabre shot. Just as he was about to press the button, however, the doctor sat up and exclaimed: "Goodness, I had almost forgotten the bird. Mr. Photographer, I want the picture to show a pretty bird kissing me as I lie dead. If you haven't a stuffed bird around here, send out and get one from the taxidermist's."

And there she calmly lay until the photographer's assistant had gone out and borrowed a stuffed hummingbird from a taxidermist's shop. The photo was then taken.

It was almost twenty years before real death came to claim Dr. Walker, and the indefatigable campaigner had many battles ahead. She witnessed the rise of the suffragette movement, the contribution that women made to World War I, and the extension of votes to women that followed. Obituaries referred to her as "the original suffragette" and before her death she received special dispensation from Congress granting the right to wear men's clothes.

Japan's Wartime Survivors

In 1972, US President Richard Nixon made a historic visit to China, which opened a new era in East-West relations; it was also the year in which Palestinian terrorists disrupted the Munich Olympics, and the year of Francis Ford Coppola's blockbuster film *The Godfather*. Man had long since walked on the moon, and the women's liberation movement was already a force to be reckoned with.

And yet, for a lonely recluse hiding out on the Pacific island of Guam, it was as if World War II had never ended. On January 26, the *Times* reported:

"A Japanese soldier who remained faithful to his orders never to surrender was captured yesterday after twenty-eight years of hiding.

"Sergeant Shoichi Yokoi, now fifty-six, was surprised at nightfall by two hunters in the heavily wooded Talofo River district, twenty miles from Agana, while on his way to the river to set a trap for fish. They covered him with their rifles and marched him to a police station."

Yokoi was heavily bearded when found, wearing trousers and a jacket made from tree and bark. He had been a tailor before the war that started in 1941 and used a pair of scissors he had throughout the war to shape the clothes and to cut his hair. He told reporters that he had lived since the war on a diet of nuts, breadfruit, mangoes, papaya, shrimp, snails, rats, and frogs. He had never heard of either of the atomic bombs, or of television, and stared in disbelief when told that a jet aircraft could return him to his hometown of Nagoya in three hours.

For twenty-eight years, Sergeant Yokoi had lived in a time warp. He told reporters that he and two other Japanese citizens fled into the jungles of Guam when American troops recaptured the island in 1944. They knew that on Guam, at least, the war was over, because of leaflets they found scattered through the jungle.

But of the larger dimension, they were quite ignorant. Yokoi and his two comrades held out, fearing they might be executed if they surrendered: "We dug a cave in a bamboo thicket hut and after a few months our food ran out. The others moved to a new hiding place where there was more food. We visited each other." About eight years before his discovery, Yokoi had gone to the cave where the others were living and found them dead. "I believe they died of starvation," he said. Yokoi himself had been ill several times: "I caught a pig and apparently did not cook it very well. Another time I became numb and feared I was starving."

Yokoi had burned his service uniform on orders. Besides his tailor's scissors, the only relics he kept from his army days were a waistband embroidered by his mother and a Japanese flag, both of which he had hidden in the cave. "I stayed close to the cave all the time I was in the jungle," he said. "I never went out except at night and always stayed in the same area." The two hunters had almost bumped into him in the dark.

Speaking of the future, he said: "I would like to be reunited with my family and then go up a mountain and meditate for a long time." In fact, he had only one surviving blood relative, whose wife informed reporters that the family had been told in September 1944 that Yokoi had been killed "somewhere in the Pacific." Before being transferred to Guam in 1943, his parents had arranged a marriage for him. Yokoi had no idea if his fiancée was even alive.

Doctors at a Guam hospital said that Yokoi's blood pressure, heart, and pulse were normal, but he seemed to be anemic as a result of his salt-free diet. Arrangements were made for his return to Japan as soon as his health permitted. "This is like a dream to me," said the soldier. "I am only afraid I will wake up."

After the initial reports, the press filled in some of the details. It appeared that Yokoi was the third former Japanese soldier to have been found on Guam long after the war was over; two others had been discovered sixteen years earlier.

Yokoi was entitled to back pay and allowances for his lonely years of struggle in the jungle, which wound up being only a very small amount of money.

Yokoi's story struck disturbing chords in the Japanese imagination, echoing largely forgotten values of samurai loyalty and discipline. And if Japan was haunted by Yokoi's experience, so was the survivor himself'. In the Guam hospital where he was being cared for, he suffered nightmares about the spirits of departed comrades who scolded him for planning to return to Japan alone.

Yokoi slept only fitfully, crouching against a wall in a position that recalled the way he had slept in his jungle hideout. During the day, he brooded, holding his head in his hands. He broke out into cold sweats and muttered that a ghost was standing at his bedside, admonishing him for having deserted

Imperial Japanese Army soldier Shoichi Yokoi finally returned home after hiding out on the island of Guam for twenty-eight years.

his comrades. Doctors were alarmed about his mental condition. A Japanese journalist reported: "He seems to be making a desperate effort to find an exit from the 'time tunnel' that separates his former world from today's civilization."

Guam itself had now become a popular resort for Japanese tourists. When Yokoi saw honeymooning couples, the men with long hair, the girls in hot pants, he stared in disbelief. "Are they really Japanese?" he asked.

The reporters themselves were an enigma to him. "You are different Japanese," he said. "There must be other Japanese people."

Eventually, the doctors considered him fit enough to leave the hospital and return to Japan. He was brought back on an aircraft, which also bore home the ashes of his two comrades, who had died of starvation. Yokoi's return was a nationally televised event that aroused intense curiosity.

About five thousand people gathered at the airport. Among them were many veterans of the old Imperial Army. One, dressed in his former uniform, held up a banner declaring: "Only Mr. Yokoi still possesses the Spirit of Japan." An official reception, headed by the welfare minister, was at hand. Yokoi emerged unsteadily from the aircraft, supported by medical attendants and waving a pink hand towel to acknowledge flag waving and cries of "Banzai" from the crowd. On arrival, the remains of his comrades, contained in white boxes, were presented to weeping relatives.

At a crowded press conference held later, Yokoi looked tired and drawn but surprisingly fit. Questions had been carefully prepared by Japanese journalists, inviting the former soldier to express his feelings on returning and to make suitably appropriate comments about the horrors of war. To their embarrassment, Yokoi appeared not to share the expected sentiments. He was ashamed to come back, he said, and his sole purpose was to give a full report on what happened at Guam as this might be useful if Japan had to fight another war.

Yokoi spoke in dry, staccato sentences. Only when mention was made of the emperor did his voice break with emotion: "I am terribly ashamed that I was not able to serve His Majesty satisfactorily," he said, wiping away tears. He was shocked, too, that the emperor should be treated in the media like an ordinary person. By the standards of his pre-war youth, these were "sacrilegious things."

The whole affair had touched nerves in Japanese society, recalling the ancient code of service, the shame of surrender, and the law of unquestioning obedience to a semi-divine emperor. What part had they to play in a Japan whose international standing no longer depended on military might but on commercial and industrial ingenuity?

Yokoi was taken to a Tokyo hospital, where he remained for some time after his sensational return. On February 5, 1972, the *Times* reported him to be in good physical condition despite dropsy in the legs. He refused to read newspapers or to watch television, which he considered too noisy. Instead, he watched his first fall of snow in more than thirty years.

A Japanese daily noted that Yokoi was the 3,107,404th soldier to return alive from World War II. And yet, incredibly, he was not the last.

For many years after the war, Philippine police had reported occasional gun battles involving its forces on the island of Lubang and a group of renegade Japanese soldiers. One had surrendered in 1950. Another was killed in a shootout with Philippine police in 1954. A third was shot dead in 1972, the very year of Yokoi's discovery. A fourth, however, was believed to be alive. His name was even known: Lieutenant Hiroo Onoda.

At a cost of $400,000 the Japanese Welfare Ministry tried to persuade him that the war was over and that he should come home. Search parties were sent out, loudspeakers were used, and leaflets dropped from the air. Onoda remained in the jungle, a mysterious recluse sighted occasionally in his Japanese uniform. When the search parties came too close, he fired from hidden positions.

Finally, in February 1974, a young Japanese adventurer named Norio Suzuki went to Lubang to hunt down the renegade. His policy was cautious; instead of attempting to track the gunman to his lair, he set up camp in a jungle clearing known to be on Onoda's "patch" and waited for his quarry to find him. Eventually, Onoda turned up. Suzuki told him of the concern his case was causing in Japan, but Onoda was resolute. He would return, he said, only if his commanding officer withdrew his order to go on fighting.

Suzuki communicated the news to the authorities who managed to get hold of former Major Yoshimi Taniguchi, a Kyushu bookseller, sixty-three years of age, who had been Onoda's last military superior. The bookseller was flown to Lubang, where an extraordinary meeting took place.

"Lieutenant Onoda reporting for duty, sir!" said the renegade, dressed in a battered cap and a tattered uniform, and still clutching his old regulation infantry rifle. He stood to attention as Taniguchi read out an Imperial Army order dating from September 1945: "As of this moment, all officers and men under this command shall terminate all hostilities."

Onoda bowed stiffly, acknowledging at last that his war was over. He then proceeded to brief his former commander about nearly thirty years of intelligence gathered on "enemy movements."

Onoda's story was rather different from that of Sergeant Yokoi, who had been afraid and uncertain about whether the war was over. Onoda, in contrast, knew what the position was. During his years in hiding, he had listened on a stolen transistor radio to the Japanese language service of the BBC. He had heard the loudspeaker addresses and read the leaflets addressed to him. But despite all, he had remained faithful to the code of the imperial field service.

Onoda had been posted to Lubang late in 1944, as a graduate of the army intelligence school. His orders were very clear: "To continue carrying out your mission even after the Japanese Army surrenders, no matter what happens." When the island was liberated by American and Philippine forces, Onoda went into hiding with three compatriots. One after another, they had surrendered or died. Onoda kept on fighting.

The Year of the Trespasser

The US Secret Service suffered embarrassment in 2014, which was dubbed the "year of the trespasser." That's because five different people managed to get past White House security and make it through the presidential gates. And while none sat on the president's bed in the middle of the night, it was still considered a major security breach.

Four of the trespassers scaled the fence and jumped over right before security forces. The fifth may have been the most embarrassing–a toddler managed to squeeze between the bars of the fence and wander onto the property.

The little guy was corralled by secret service agents and returned to his parents. The incident was not without consequence, however, as the area had to be put on lockdown, which delayed an import television address that President Obama was scheduled to deliver to the American people.

He established a series of hideouts across the 74-square-mile (191-sq-km) island, stealing food and keeping several caches of live ammunition intact. Like Yokoi, he had known the fear of starvation, and like Yokoi he improvised clothing, using bits of old tires for sandals. He had, however, kept his uniform intact by patching it with plants where necessary. His sense of duty was even more marked than Yokoi's; over the years, he and his men were suspected of having killed at least thirty Philippine islanders and wounding a further one hundred.

After the meeting with Taniguchi, Onoda was taken to Manila where he formally presented his rusty samurai sword to the Philippine president, Ferdinand Marcos, to acknowledge his surrender. The president pardoned him, even adding: "You're a great soldier."

Onoda's return to Japan was even more emotional than Yokoi's. *Time* magazine referred to "Hiroo worship." Again, thousands turned up at Tokyo airport, while press helicopters swarmed above.

The shame and distress which Yokoi had exhibited did not appear to affect Onoda. He greeted the praise of his countrymen with philosophical calm.

At the press conference he was asked what had been his toughest experience during his long years of struggle. 'To have lost my comrades in arms,' he replied. And the most pleasant experience?

"Nothing—nothing pleasant happened to me through all those twenty-nine years."

The Palace Intruder

The *Daily Express*, which broke the story, called it "the most gross and scandalous lapse of security in her thirty-year reign."

Queen Elizabeth II of England had, one early morning in 1982, been abruptly awakened by an intruder at Buckingham Palace. The man was barefoot, wearing jeans and a T-shirt. He had sat on her bed cradling a broken ashtray in his hands and dripped blood onto the royal sheets.

For an eerie ten minutes, the man had engaged his sovereign in conversation, making no threatening moves but preferring to chat about the coincidence that each of them had four children. The queen was finally saved when a chambermaid entered the royal bedroom, took one look at the prowler, and blurted: "Bloody hell, Ma'am! What's he doing in here?"

What was he doing in there? How had he got into the bedroom? Where were the guards? And where, for that matter, was Prince Philip? The full story of the sensational incident emerged only over several weeks, following a police investigation and the intruder's trial on a charge quite separate from the palace break-in.

The prowler's name was Michael Fagan, aged thirty-three, an unemployed decorator from North London. Fagan was never brought to court for the incident in the royal bedroom. Instead, he was charged for an earlier indiscretion. Incredibly, Michael Fagan had been in the palace before, a month earlier, and for that offense he was charged only with stealing half a bottle of wine.

At a preliminary hearing, Fagan entered with his hands behind his back and strutted into the court. He constantly turned and smiled toward members of his family. Propping his feet on a wrought iron rail at the front of the dock, he laughed and waved to his wife and mother. Fagan appeared to be enjoying himself. Only when the name of the queen was mentioned did he bristle: "I told you not to fetch her name up," he glowered at his attorney. "I would rather plead guilty than have her name dragged into this."

Indeed, throughout the whole bizarre affair, one thing emerged very clearly: Fagan practically worshipped his monarch. Fagan told the jury that he broke into the palace on that first occasion because "a little voice in my head" told him to do so. His defense was that he did it as a favor to the queen, proving the security at the palace had lapsed.

Despite the very full account that Fagan gave of this first visit, the jury found him not guilty. It was an extraordinary decision: "Bonkers!" the *Sun* called it, in a banner headline splashed across its front page. "Next time you are walking along The Mall and feel thirsty, why not pop into Buckingham Palace for a glass or two?" it suggested. Fagan had clearly not entered the palace in order to steal the wine, but the decision remained astonishing.

It appeared that through a vagary of English law, Fagan could not be charged with trespassing for his second visit, when he entered the royal bedroom.

Fagan got inside by climbing a railing near the gates to the Ambassadors' Entrance at 6:45 a.m. He was spotted by a policeman but, in the first of a startling string of gaffes, the police control room let the warning slip.

Through an unlocked ground floor window, Fagan climbed into the Stamp Room, where the extensive royal stamp collection is displayed. An alarm was set off but it was ignored. Fagan then went back out the same window, shimmied up a drainpipe, removed his socks and sandals, and climbed in another window that had just been unlocked by a maid. For a quarter of an hour, he prowled around the palace corridors unchallenged.

One member of the palace staff remembered seeing him, but did not consider his behavior sufficiently suspicious to cause alarm. The intruder slipped through various warning devices that had been badly adjusted. Finally, he found the private apartments by "following the pictures" along the gallery that connects to the queen's quarters. In the storm of publicity that ensued, some rather offbeat discoveries were made about the domestic life of the royal family, the type of nightgown the queen wore, and that she and her husband had separate bedrooms.

The inefficiency of the security services was, of course, the subject of much outraged comment. The *Times* observed: "So much for the guards at Buckingham Palace." The newspapers dug up palace intrusions from the past and noted that lax security was not a new phenomenon. And yet Fagan's expeditions remained unique in their bizarre quality and the scandal that ensued.

Following his apprehension, Fagan remained in police custody, even after his acquittal on the wine-stealing charge. It was felt that his state of mind was such that his movements and actions were totally unpredictable. Clearly he was suffering from mental illness. A few months later he was brought to trial on a charge of stealing a car.

Although Fagan was not present for the duration of the hearing, he did leave a statement drawn up while awaiting trial. Remorseful in tone and clearly authentic in sentiment, it provided a curiously sad epitaph on the whole sensational affair:

> *Along with everyone else in the world, I love Her Majesty the Queen. I have the deepest respect, the deepest respect for her. I would do nothing to embarrass her. I know she likes to help people and I thought she would like to help me. And I have admired her for eternity.*
>
> *I understand that I should have written to her rather than gone to see her, and that by doing so I have caused her unwelcome and inaccurate publicity which I do not wish*

her to have. There is nothing I could do now to put the clock back although I wish I could. Anything that I can do to make up for the embarrassment I have caused I would do.

Your Majesty, please excuse my intrusion into your privacy—I didn't realize it would become a world topic. All I wanted to do was discuss my personal problems, but the way I went about it has embarrassed Your Majesty's family.

You were wonderfully understanding with me and I know you will accept that this apology is written with all sincerity. Humbly, Michael

CHAPTER FOUR: WEIRD STUNTS

RIDICULOUS RECORDS, FANTASTIC FEATS

The Guinness Book of World Records provides fertile ground for students of the weird, registering such feats as cucumber slicing, hot water bottle bursting, billiard table jumping, and the dropping of eggs intact from great heights. Other unpleasant events include the ever-popular spittin', Belchin', and Cussin' Triathlon.

The breaking of records in such events is generally worth a snippet in the local or national press. For example, housewife Dorothy Hall has knitted the world's longest scarf (1,332 feet [402 m] long and using 1,400 ounces [39,689 g] of wool), while in 2016, twenty Italian cheerleaders managed to squeeze into a tiny two-seat smart car to equal a record set in 2011.

Cramming twenty people into a small car can certainly be uncomfortable and cause a bout of claustrophobia but is otherwise safe. That's not the case with others. Take New York's Ashrita Furman for example. He actually holds the most Guinness records in the world including one set in 2016 in a swimming pool in Queens when he caught the most spears shot from a spear gun underwater in one minute.

However, it is often a failure, or an incidental occurrence, which stimulates extended treatment in the press. Such was the case with John Berry, who was twenty-one when he made an attempt on the snake pit endurance record. Berry had himself enclosed in a glass tank at a seaside fair with twenty-two poisonous snakes; at least, there were twenty-two at the outset. Berry had ordered a dozen cobras, but was sent ten cobras and two kraits and about a third of the way through the attempt, a cobra ate one of the kraits. Unfortunately for Berry, he was bitten by a puff adder and rushed to the hospital, ending his miserable five-week ordeal in the tank. He was only about halfway to the record!

"Voice from the Grave Proposes to Barmaid": So it was that the *Times* headlined a feature concerning an attempt on the world record for live burial, which occurred in November 1981. The story that followed was as bizarre as the macabre event. Beryl Wilson, aged thirty-seven, a bartender from Leeds, England, was to marry a man she had never met and who proposed to her from a coffin. "Wild" Bill White, her intended husband, was buried alive in a grave at Fort Worth,

Records are constantly being broken. This daredevil broke the world record for longest bicycle jump between platforms.

Texas, trying to set an endurance record for living 6 feet (182 cm) underground.

Their romance started after a radio DJ interviewed White and gave the telephone number of his coffin to Radio 1 listeners. Beryl Wilson phoned him and later received a proposal. White, who was buried alive on July 11, remained in his coffin until December 19, breaking the record by staying underground for 140 days. Remarkably, it was the sixtieth time he was buried alive.

He told the media they had overblown the romantic relationship and told them that he was receiving between five hundred and six hundred phone calls per day while buried alive!

Holland's Wim Hof, known as the "Iceman," regularly breaks records for the amount of time he can spend in icy waters. Using a combination of yoga and meditation, Hof broke his own record in 2008 by spending an hour and nearly fourteen seconds in freezing water! That hurts just writing about it.

A different kind of danger, and a different kind of run-up, were illustrated in the first annual Empire State Building marathon of February 1978. This event involved running up the 1,575 steps of the celebrated New York skyscraper and was won by a former New York fireman, August Gary Muhrcke. He beat fourteen other runners in an impressive twelve minutes and thirty-two seconds. Unfortunately, Muhrcke was faced with the loss of his disability pension. He had retired with an injury from the New York City Fire Department at the age of thirty-seven, saying his injured back would no longer allow him to work as a firefighter. Those who have overcome true disability to compete with the able-bodied, or those simply willing to do good, present rather more heroic examples of human achievement.

Dashrath Manjhi of India is one perfect example. Known simply as the "Mountain Man," Manjhi decided to literally carve a road through a mountain. You see, years earlier Manjhi's wife injured herself on the mountain and died when it took doctors too long to travel around the mountain.

Armed with simple laborer's tools, sledgehammer and pickaxe, it took Manjhi twenty-two years to carve the road, wide enough for emergency vehicles to travel through the mountain. When he was complete, this single man was able to reduce the trip for the doctors to his village from 46.5 miles (74 km) to only a few miles.

Acclaimed in his native India, Manjhi said his motivation was that no one else suffer the fate he had in losing his wife. He died in 2007 after a long bout with cancer. He died a hero.

Nasty Noshers

For many, the Fourth of July holiday has become more than a day of barbecues, fireworks, and great sales at the mall. It is also the day where we watch in amazement and disgust the annual hot dog eating contest in Coney Island, New York, where professional eaters compete to win the grand prize.

The eating frenzy consists of competitors soaking their frankfurter and bun in water to soften it before cramming the entire thing in their mouths and chewing.

The fierce competition between Joey Chestnut and Takeru Kobayashi started around 2001 and made the annual competition that started in 1916 a national spectacle. Chestnut once downed seventy hot dogs in ten minutes. Others have come close, but no one is yet to crack his record.

Others have made their marks eating, well, stuff that probably should not be eaten. In 1906, the *Daily Mirror* recorded the death of Robert Naysmith, a stuntman whose specialty was swallowing nails, hatpins, stones, glass, and other unorthodox items. Known as the Human Ostrich, Naysmith came to a predictable end. He became ill and had to give up his profession, afterwards earning a few pennies per day selling shoelaces in the streets. As his condition worsened, he sought admission to the hospital, and when he told doctors that he had been swallowing nails and hatpins for a living, understandably, they did not believe him at first.

He asked for a knife to relieve himself of one item. The doctors considered him crazy and placed him under close observation. Then an abscess formed on his body. When it was opened, a brass-headed nail was found inside.

Too weak to endure an operation, Naysmith became worse and died. At the postmortem, more than thirty nails and hatpins were found in his body—some in the liver, some in the kidneys, and most in the intestines.

The case of the Human Ostrich ought to have provided a salutary warning to all aspiring successors in his line of business. But it hasn't. In December 1969, for example, the *Sunday Express* carried the story of "The Man who is Eating a Bus." Milovije Ristic, a twenty-six-year-old Serb from Bor, near the former Yugoslav-Bulgarian border, had bought an old bus and planned to eat it all over the course of two years. Ristic had already swallowed 22,500 razor blades, a ton of glass, hundreds of knives and forks, chains, nuts, bolts, and other items of ironware. Asked about indigestion he replied: "Nothing a handful of ball bearings wouldn't cure."

In September 1982, the same newspaper wrote about how Alan Newbold's appetite for "ghastly grub" had led to divorce after twenty-five years of happy marriage. Newbold was described as the World Nasty Nosh champion. The years of serving up such delicacies as sheep's eyes and pigs' brains had taken their toll on his wife, Mary. But Newbold was undeterred. "In November," the *Sun* announced, "he flies to America to eat a crushed-up bicycle on a TV show."

His eating habits paled in comparison to Frenchmen Michel Lotito, nicknamed, "The Man Who Eats It All." Lotito, who claimed never to have become sick from his eating habits, consumed bicycles, shopping carts, and even a small airplane before his death in 2007. His trick, he said, was to

Michel Lotito, also known as Monsieur Mangetout, never met a piece of metal he wouldn't eat.

cut the metal into small pieces and drink lots of water and mineral water every day!

In October 1963, the *British Medical Journal* contained an interesting note of nasty noshing in its correspondence columns: "The biggest collection of foreign material that I have ever heard of was published in the Sunday *Pictorial* of September 21, 1958, when it was said that a surgeon in Sweden had at one operation removed:1,500 pins and needles, 330 buttons, 167 coins, 12 curtain rings, 11 keys, and 176 other things including fishhooks, badges, nails, stones, a buckle, and a bicycle tire valve!"

On July 20, 1981, Mel Harvey, a professional stuntman, jumped 125 feet (38 m) from the top of a block of apartments in England, landing in a 10-foot-high (3 m) pile of cardboard boxes.

The feat was over in a few seconds; his speed on impact was estimated at 60 miles per hour (96 km/h). Was it a record? Nobody knew. Harvey had performed the jump for charity to raise money for a new treatment hospital. He landed quite safely and did not require hospital treatment himself.

Compared with the feats of freefall parachutists, of course, Harvey's jump was a very modest affair. The youngest contender in this perilous field was once little Devorie Beck from Florida. Devorie was just twenty-three months old when she made her first parachute jump. It was over 12,000 feet (3,657 m) and, amazingly, the first 7,500 feet (2,286) were freefall.

"Skybaby" Devorie jumped attached by a special harness to her father, Jim, a Florida miner. Of her first plunge through space she declared, "We had fun. We had fun." Indeed, she is so relaxed that she even clutches a lollipop as she falls.

By her father's account, Devorie started asking to be taken on a jump as soon as she could talk. "It's my turn," she would tell him every time she saw him land. Jim Beck, an experienced skydiver with over a thousand jumps to his credit, eventually got an extra-large parachute to satisfy her demands: "If for one moment she had changed her mind or hesitated, I wouldn't have jumped with her," he said. But wasn't it risky? "I would never take her if I was not 100 percent sure there was no risk,'" he said.

In recent years thrill-seekers have traded in their parachutes for outfits resembling that of a flying squirrel, known as a wingsuit. These daredevils jump from buildings and mountains and —most of the time—manage to glide at speeds of 100 miles per hour (160 km/h), directing their own path before either pulling a parachute cord or crash landing onto a soft landing pad.

But the adrenaline junkies have taken the sport and made it even more dangerous by including gliding as close to cliffs and mountainsides as they can and gliding for longer and longer distances before pulling their chords. Controversy erupted in 2013 when a string of these wingsuit deaths occurred.

The rumblings of discontent started a year earlier in 2012, when Frenchman Herve le Gallou, a true pioneer of the sport crashed and died during a jump. Over the next year twenty-two jumpers would perish and some called the activity more suicide than sport.

Still, hundreds continue to take part. There is even a professional wingsuit league now in China.

Freak Show

Throughout the history of entertainment, physical freaks and prodigies have been exhibited by enterprising showmen. At a fair in 1814, for example, a fireproof lady was put on display. Her stunts included putting melted lead into her mouth and spitting it out marked with her teeth. She passed a red-hot iron over her body and limbs, her tongue and her hair, thrust her arm into fire, and washed her hands, not only in boiling lead but also in boiling oil and water, all apparently without ill effect.

Angelo Faticoni was a total enigma to medical authorities. Known as the Human Cork, he performed extraordinary feats of buoyancy in front of students and professors at Harvard University. The experts believed that his internal organs were not as those of other men, but they found no special evidence to confirm their theory. An obituary for "The Man They Could Not Drown" was published in the *New York Herald Times* in 1931, recalling that Faticoni could stay afloat in the water for fifteen hours with 20 pounds (9 kg) of lead tied to his ankles. Moreover:

> *Faticoni could sleep in water, roll up in a ball, lie on his side, or assume any position asked of him. Once he was sewn into a bag and then thrown into the water, with a twenty-pound cannonball lashed to his legs. His head reappeared on the surface soon afterward, and he remained motionless in that position for eight hours. Another time he swam across the Hudson tied to a chair weighted with lead.*

Faticoni died aged seventy-two, taking his secret with him to the grave, an enigma to medics and laymen alike.

Dwarves and giants have always fascinated the public. The most celebrated dwarf was Charles Sherwood Stratton, born in 1838. Billed as "General Tom Thumb," he was exhibited in Barnum's famous circus, measuring 1 foot 4 inches (40.64 cm). His fame rested more on his flair for the theater than on a truly exceptional shortness: he played Napoleon I and Frederick the Great and went about London in a blue and white carriage drawn by Shetland ponies. Even in his own lifetime, however, he was undercut by William E. Jackson, known as Major Mite, who measured only 21 inches (53 cm) at the age of sixteen, in 1880. Major Mite was exhibited in England at this time in the company of Lucia Zarate, seventeen years old and an inch shorter (both grew to exceed the generally accepted world record).

At the other end of the scale stood record-breaking giant Robert Pershing Wadlow, who was nearly 9 feet (274 cm) tall, measuring 8 feet and 11 inches (271 cm) at the time of his death in 1940. He has had his competitors, however; among them, the 8-foot-tall (96 cm) Captain Martin Van Buren Bates, the

Subliminal Crackers

The word "sex" is shallowly implanted in the molds that are used to make Ritz crackers, according to American consumer watchdog Bryan Key. The three letters are supposed to be visible on the salted side, stimulating hungry consumers to buy and eat more Ritz. Ritz manufacturers, however, deny that there is any sex in the biscuits at all.

—*Sunday Times*

"Kentucky Giant" who fought for the Confederates during the Civil War and was promoted to captain at the age of sixteen.

ADVERTISING GIMMICKS

In 1977, a bizarre legal battle broke out in the United States between the self-proclaimed president of a nonexistent country and the New York Telephone Company. The case revolved around sixteen entries in the Manhattan telephone directory under the general heading, "Montmartre, Government of."

The entries included the Montmartre International War Crimes Commission, the Montmartre Military Mission to the Kurds, the Commission to Internationalize the Vatican City State, and the Montmartre Military Mission to the Royal Scottish Jacobite Government. The entries had been made by Barry Richmond, who claimed to rule sixteen million people within a 500-hundred-square-mile (1,294-sq-km) territory in New York State.

The New York Telephone Company was not amused and planned to cut the entries from the next year's directory. Richmond protested and warned: "I told the man from the Phone Company that if I caught any telephone men on my territory out of uniform I would have them hanged as spies."

In fact, the whole affair was a publicity stunt. Richmond, a theatrical promoter, had plans to revive in the United States the once-celebrated French theater of the grotesque, the Grand Guignol, which was listed as his republic's national theater.

The history of advertising is rich in weird stunts designed to get a product known—at whatever cost. In the early nineteenth century, for example, a huge, horsedrawn top hat, mounted on springs, plied London streets advertising Perring's Light Hats. With advances in technology, new possibilities opened up. In 1893, a cloud projector was erected at the Chicago Exhibition, beaming into the heavens statistics of how many people had visited the fair during the day. The idea was also adopted to advertise *Picture* magazine.

During the interwar period (the years between World War I and World War II), pilots developed the art of skywriting with trails of smoke. There was even a vogue for sky-shouting. "Suddenly you will hear a voice from heaven shouting 'Smoke Old Gold,' and then you will hear a bit of music," protested one victim, adding: "It is very discouraging to any mental application."

The sky was the limit—the ultimate hoarding—and its use for advertising aroused bitter controversy. When asked whether the public could really be expected to enjoy reading such messages as "Buy Baxter's Pills and Cure Constipation" in the heavens, one irate inventor protested: "I often wonder why it is that when approaching this question my opponents always think of the most beastly kind of slogan."

Yet the question was not entirely unfair. Newspaper readers had long grown accustomed to the proud boasts of laxative manufacturers in their dailies—why not in the sky? Medical products had been zealously promoted since the earliest days of the press. In the eighteenth century, worm powders were especially prominent, and manufacturers organized lurid public displays to entice customers. One man, Mr. Moore, for example, informed readers of the British Weekly *Mercury* of January 29, 1715 that:

> *This day a Young Gentlewoman had a Worm brought away sixteen foot and Odd Inches long ... This, with several others of Prodigious Size are to be seen at the said Mr. Moore's, viz. One of thirty Foot long, another five and a half, being part of one sixteen Yards odd inches; another six Yards and a half, another fifty Foot, and another in the form of a Bird, but very small.*

Curious indeed were some of the items advertised in the nineteenth-century press.

For ladies, for example, there was a Dimple-Making Machine, consisting of a knife "with a dainty but very sharp blade, a tiny keen-edged scoop, and a very fine needle." With these instruments, it was alleged, "a pretty, life-like dimple can be produced as effective as the genuine print of the 'angel's kiss.'"

For gentlemen, the *Penny Magazine* of 1909 advertised the only patent Nose Machines in the world: "Improve ugly noses of all kinds. Can be worn during sleep." Ugly ears? "My patent Rubber Ear Caps remedy ugly outstanding ears." "We Buy Old or Disused False Teeth," declared an Ipswich firm in the *Penny Pictorial*.

With such extraordinary claims being made daily in the newspapers, were aerial laxatives such an unthinkable proposition?

Sometimes, an advertising campaign may go disastrously wrong. For several months through the summer of 1982, Lever Brothers of New York distributed free samples of Sunlight, a dishwashing liquid, in bright yellow plastic bottles with lemons on the label. The pale liquid oozed out, exuding an extraordinarily authentic scent of freshly-cut lemons.

Unfortunately, people reported nausea, vomiting, and diarrhea shortly after using the product. They had taken it to be concentrated lemon juice and used it to flavor iced tea, salads, and fish. In all, some 2,500 people made the same mistake. Happily nobody died–the director of the National Poison Center in Pittsburgh commented: "You'd have to drown in it first." But the symptoms were not pleasant.

In 1977, an enterprising New York bookstore mounted a much more successful campaign. It placed a large advertisement in the *New York Times*, asking: "Ever been kissed in a bookstore before?" The ad went on to guarantee that anyone who bought a paperback called *The Art of Kissing* would be rewarded with an expert kiss.

A stand was set up at the shop and a man and a woman stood ready to deliver. Customers who bought the book were presented with a paper token and, armed with it, went to the male or female attendant, according to preference. "More people came to watch than to take part," the *Times* noted. "The shop was crammed with voyeurs, and others were standing two and three deep on the pavement outside, peering through the window. Flashlights were set up, and photographers took photos as the courageous few made their way to the stand."

Hardly an intimate event, but then it is not the business of the promoter to be discreet. Pan Am staff at London's Heathrow Airport were once faced with a most embarrassing request. In order to "underscore our commitment to achieve the finest degree possible of personalized service," the president of Pan American World Airways developed a great idea. Huge shiny lapel buttons with musical notes printed on them were issued to hundreds of porters, cashiers, and stewardesses. There was no text—just a dozen or so notes.

As puzzled customers asked what the notes meant, beaming employees were supposed to burst forth into song: "Pan Am makes the going—and makes it great!"

However, when the president of Pan Am flew into the airport, he was disappointed to find that the staff was not complying with the scheme. In fact, only the shame-faced station manager was wearing a badge. "It's ridiculous," an airport worker told reporters. "I wouldn't dream of wearing this huge button. It looks crazy."

The plan was quietly dropped, along with another of the president's ideas: an all-American college choir singing jingles to greet passengers at the airport.

How are these daft ideas dreamed up? In 1980, Barry Goldwater Jr., a California member of the House of Representatives, put forward a most ingenious plan. Forget the giant neon displays, the skywriting, and the multiple hoardings.

Goldwater's scheme was in one sense much more grandiose. He proposed legislation permitting companies to have their brand names printed on US postage stamps.

Sportswear and racing cars were already awash with brand names. Why not stamps? The plan was carefully planned out: the fee for advertising would be 20 cents a stamp. In total, the idea would produce $1,200 in revenue for the US Post Office.

American philatelists were furious, claiming that their country would become a laughing stock. The nation's twenty-five million stamp collectors would be up in arms, warned the editor of a leading philatelists' magazine. Again the old objections were raised. What would you get? George Washington's head, and beneath it: "Buy Baxter's Pills and Cure Constipation"?

The plan was not adopted. Goldwater, however, was very proud of his brainchild. "The idea just came into my head while I was taking a shower," he said. "That's where I do my best thinking."

Some weird-sounding plans however do work. In 2010, the Museum of Science and Industry in Chicago was eager to draw more people to the museum, which had fallen on difficult times.

The board of directors decided to have a contest in which the winner would get to live at the museum, in an exhibit on display, for a full month. They would be able to talk about their experiences every day on social media and would earn a check of $10,000 after the month.

They expected a few hundred entries in the essay contest but received nearly two thousand. The contest was reported on nationally and the patronage at the museum rose so significantly they held a second contest a few years later.

CHAPTER FIVE: RELIGION AND THE OCCULT

THE POWERS OF LIGHT AND DARKNESS

Fanaticism, both occult and religious, continues to provide the press with weird tales in an age generally regarded as faithless. The most sensational case of Satanism in recent years was undoubtedly that of Charles Manson, the hippy "messiah" who sent his disciples to kill actress Sharon Tate in the summer of 1969. Manson, an ex-convict and failed pop singer, headed a commune known as the "Family" in the arid California desert. Followers lived an existence of squalid promiscuity; Manson demanded that female disciples copulate with any visitor he chose. The ghastly details of the Hollywood killings sent a shiver through the whole California hippy community—in a sense they brought the era of peace and love to an end.

More offbeat allegations of Satanic practice were reported in 1982 and directed at the perfectly respectable company of Procter and Gamble, makers of such familiar household items as Charmin, Pampers, and Tide.

"Satan Is Creeping Into Your Kitchen!" alleged printed handouts issued by a Baptist group. "The rumors are so preposterous as to be laughable, were the implications not so serious," countered a company spokesman. "It is very strange the way such a ridiculous tale is taken seriously and then spreads so quickly."

The allegations revolved around the company's famous trademark, representing the man in the moon. Some evangelical Christians claimed that the figure represented the ram, one of the Devil's supposed incarnations. The symbol was also al-

The disciples of cult leader Charles Manson murdered pregnant Hollywood actress Sharon Tate.

leged to contain the infamous number 666, described in the Book of Revelation as a sign of the Great Beast, or Antichrist. It was found possible to make 666 appear by connecting the stars in the trademark—the curls at the bottom of the sign were also supposed to form a mirror image of the number.

By June of 1982, the company was receiving fifteen thousand complaints a month about the supposed Satanic pact, and Procter and Gamble took legal action against four individuals alleged to have spread the story. Ironically, the firm has a reputation of being particularly straightlaced.

Obsession with demons is as old as faithar and has made its appearance in the newspapers throughout the twentieth century. In 1925, the *St. Louis Star* reported:

> *A large man industriously rubbing the head of a smaller man at Broadway and Market Street attracted the attention of Detective Sergeant Behnken.*
>
> *"Do you feel relief?" asked the large man. The small man announced that he did not, and in addition demanded help, aid, and succor.*
>
> *"What is this?" inquired Behnken.*
>
> *"Very simple," said the large man. "This poor fellow has demons. I am taking them out of him."*

"Have you got demons?" asked Behnken.
"I have not," said the small man. "This bird grabbed me as I was walking down the street and began to rub my head."

Behnken settled the matter by giving the demon hunter a swift kick. If demons are prone to make their appearance in unlikely settings, so, too, are angels. A curious series of reports were filed in Bavaria in the 1980s. In a typical incident, a thirty-year-old woman told police at Rosenheim that a young hitchhiker she picked up on the road to Salzburg had calmly introduced himself as the archangel Gabriel. He informed her that the world would end in 1984, and then disappeared.

She insisted that the archangel had vanished without trace from her speeding car. "One moment he was there and the next there was just the empty seatbelt," declared the awe-struck woman. Police said: "The woman was visibly shaken and gave a very credible impression."

At least six similar reports of the elusive angel had been made in Bavaria during the previous year, and the Catholic Church there was prompted to issue a press statement, reassuring the public that the mystery hitchhiker could not possibly be the archangel Gabriel. "It is inconceivable that an angel would every appear in the form of a hitchhiker," said a spokesman. "And it is not in the interests of God to issue such a message of doom."

By tradition, it is through the Bible that the Christian faith is normally communicated.

The Bible remains the world's best-selling book, and there has always been money to be made out of the sacred word. Devout Christians blanched to discover in 1981 that *Reader's Digest* was planning a condensed version of the Bible, and more than one newspaper speculated waggishly as to which of the Ten Commandments were to be omitted. The potted Bible was published in 1982. In all, some 320,000 words had been cut. Gone were a tenth of the words of Jesus, a quarter of the New Testament, and half of the Old. All Ten Commandments were still there, however, and so was the much-loved 23rd Psalm, only now it was the 13th.

THE RECTOR OF STIFFKEY

Among all the colorful clerics who have made their fleeting appearances in the pages of the press, none have quite competed for style with the Reverend Harold Davidson, the rector of Stiffkey. Even the name of Stiffkey, the small parish in England he served for twenty-six years, seemed to hint at the saucy potential of the saga.

The story broke in February 1932, with the news that Davidson was to be brought to trial on charges relating to his

Reverend Harold Davidson, the rector of Stiffkey, was photographed with his daughter after his trial.

moral conduct. The rector had made many trips to Soho, London's vice center, where he was counseling young girls who were in danger of falling into prostitution. This was a worthy enterprise by any standards. What troubled the church establishment was that Davidson had been bringing some of these unfortunates back to Stiflkey, even holding pajama parties for them in the rectory. Moreover, several girls charged him with attempted rape, or at least "pestering."

Davidson firmly proclaimed his innocence, claiming his interest in the girls was entirely fatherly. In the weeks leading up to the trial he continued to deliver sermons from his pulpit implicitly condemning the hypocrisy of the church hierarchy. Had not Christ Himself walked with scarlet women? "God does not wait to minister to a few saved souls– those icebergs of untempted chastity," he reminded a packed congregation at one evening service.

"Stiflkey's Rector Cheered by his Flock," headlined the *Daily Express* on the following morning. And indeed, throughout the coming trial both press and public were to remain generally favorable to the embattled rector.

Eventually, Davidson was found guilty, unfrocked, and disgraced.

The true weirdness emerged only afterward, as the ex-rector used his acting talents to pay for the cost of his defense.

He began by having himself exhibited on a beach, fasting and encased in a barrel. There was a window in the side, which allowed him to converse with paying customers as they filed past. In one mood he might mutter somberly from within: "I should like it to be known that every fiber of my being revolts against the indignity of this procedure." In another his showman's instincts took over and he might boom: "Hurry! Hurry! Hurry! See the one and only ex-rector of Stiffkey, not even the Archbishop of Canterbury can muzzle him! Hurry! Hurry! Hurry!"

Sometimes he remained entirely silent, poring over his law books and planning revenge on the church authorities. Outside the barrel, posters declared: "The former rector of Stiffkey has been placed in the present position by the authorities of the Church of England who failed in their Christian duty towards him ... The lower he sinks, the greater the crime."

The act was billed as "Fast to Death" and the police arrested him on a charge of attempting suicide by starvation. Davidson was found not guilty and was awarded damages in court. His defense had been that he had no intention of fasting to death—he could not be blamed for the show owner's advertisements. (Attendance at the barrel dropped dramatically when the ex-rector's defense was reported; customers were particularly disappointed by rumors that Davidson was not even fasting, but kept nourished by furtive supplies of grapes and bananas.)

The barrel was comfortably fitted out with a cushioned seat, electric light, and a chimney that permitted him to smoke his favorite cigars. He returned to it several times after forays elsewhere to vary his means of exhibition.

Once, for example, he was exhibited in the company of a dead whale. On another occasion he was displayed being frozen in a refrigerated chamber; on yet another he was roasted in a glass oven while a mechanical demon prodded his posterior with a pitchfork. Tireless in his ingenuity, he even appeared clad only in a loin cloth, lying on a bed of nails.

Compared with such exertions, a stint in the barrel was a profoundly relaxing experience—most of the time. Once, his fellow entertainers dropped a mouse into the barrel. Davidson had a neurotic fear of most animals and became frenzied with terror, hammering on the walls until he was let out.

Considering his phobia, Davidson's final act was one of great courage. At a sideshow, he exhibited himself in a 14-by-8-foot (4-m-by- 2-m) cage with Freddie and Toto, a pair of lions.

The act began with the ex-rector standing outside the cage, while the lions lurked behind. Davidson would deliver a ten-minute address to the public on the infamous legal judgment which had brought him so low. He would end with a few quips, to the effect that the lions must be getting pretty tired of his speech by now, and "I don't know what they will do to me tonight."

Then, armed with a short whip, he would enter the cage for a three-minute stint with the beasts.

On the night of Wednesday July 28, 1937, the ex-rector's long saga, which had provided sensational newspaper copy for over half a decade, reached its tragic and fittingly bizarre climax. That evening, as he entered the cage, the lions were unusually drowsy. Davidson began to flick his whip at them, encouraging them to "get a move on." Toto, the lioness, barely stirred. But Freddie, the male, quickened and began to prowl around the cage after his persecutor. Suddenly, the lion leapt and bowled Davidson over. There followed scenes of unimaginable horror.

A female lion tamer, Irene Somner, aged sixteen, was standing outside the cage, waiting in attendance. "I got in the cage and tried to drag the lion out," she said, "but it dragged him to a corner and we couldn't move him until the lion dropped him." Norman Wallace, a fairground assistant, described how Davidson fought furiously with the lion but could not shake him off. There was only one pole long enough to go through the bars and it was hidden underneath the cage.

Most of the audience had bolted with panic, but William Bliss, a Watford clerk, watched as the ex-rector was "carried round the den as a cat does a mouse."

Inside the cage, the female lion tamer "grasped a wooden handle, and as the lion came within reach I managed to jam it into its mouth, but it broke. Then I used an iron bar, but could not reach the lion." The girl, who was holding the beast with one hand, hit it repeatedly on the head with the other and eventually separated them.

Too late, alas. Harold Davidson was rushed to the hospital in critical condition. He died there on July 30.

And so the saga ended. Or almost ended. Following the grand traditions of stage, it remained for the show to go on. Even as Davidson lay dying in the hospital, a huge poster was set up outside the fateful pavilion, advertising two of the three principal actors in the drama:

See the Lion
that mauled and injured the Rector
and the Plucky Girl
who went to his Rescue

On the day that Davidson breathed his last, the pavilion was closed. However, Fred Rye, the proprietor, told a *Daily Express* reporter: "We shall be open for business tomorrow. We expect to get a big bank holiday crowd. The rector's name will still be used. We shall have a nice, sympathetic notice outside the booth, and people will be invited to pay to see the lion that mauled the rector and caused his death. The rector was a sportsman. I'm sure he wouldn't mind."

Friday the Thirteenth

On November 13, 1981, Robert Renphrey stayed in bed. The date fell on a Friday, notoriously bad luck. He claimed to be the most accident-prone man in Britain. During the previous five years, the fifty-three-year-old bus conductor had been involved in five car crashes and four bus breakdowns, had fallen into a river, been knocked down by a motorcycle, and had walked through a plate glass window.

Crazy Cults

An Irishman whose followers claim he once restored his pet goldfish to life set up business as god, and parents and local religious leaders grew concerned at the support he was attracting from young people. The man claimed to be "the greatest incarnation of God in the history of man—a true Perfect Master."

Allegedly besotted followers were required to repeat an incantatory sequence of words over and over again in attempts to summon up a one-thousand-petal lotus flower that was said to appear as a burning bush. One parent said: "It really is a most pernicious organization. It is causing much distress." It was not clear what part three garden gnomes, squatting at the rear of the master's garden, played in the rites.

As if to counter the growing encroachments of science, an extraordinary number of weird cults have proliferated in recent years. The sects' practices and beliefs may appear laughable to outsiders; and yet, to parents and relatives of youthful disciples, their innocence is often deeply disturbing.

Among the most famous is the Unification Church of Korean-born Reverend Sun Myung Moon. Amazing scenes were witnessed in July 1982, when more than two thousand couples were married in New York's Madison Square Garden all chosen for each other by the cult leader. The mass Moonie wedding took place in front of a football-crowd sized congregation, and following the practices of the sect, none of the individuals who exchanged wedding rings had ever seen each other before. Moon, passing through the ecstatic crowd, merely motioned brides and grooms to come forward together and gently pushed them onto the road to marriage. "I put my trust in the Reverend Moon to find my ideal partner," said one bride. "When he put us together for that first time, I was completely overcome with fear. Suddenly, here was the man I was going to spend the rest of my life with. But I looked at

Tens of thousands of couples were wed by the Reverend Sun Myung Moon at a group wedding ceremony in Madison Square Garden.

Richard and said simply: 'There's nothing to talk about, it's fine with me.'"

One of the more unique religious cults over the years is the Raelian Movement, started by a Frenchman named Rael who used to be a cabaret singer and racecar driver. That was before he met an alien named Yahweh, who revealed to him the origin of man and also promised him the use of futuristic robots.

In 2002 the group announced they had successfully cloned a human, a boast that proved to be untrue.

Of course, unusual cults are not a new phenomenon. For example, newspaper readers gaped at the exploits of Canadian-born Aimee Semple McPherson. She founded her Four Square Gospel in Los Angeles in the 1920s and employed all the pizzazz of Hollywood's golden age to spreading her message of enlightenment. At her million-dollar Angelus Temple, services were accompanied by the music of recorded choirs. Aimee would appear robed in white and parade under spotlights down a circular ramp to denounce the "Gorilla of Ungodliness."

Stranger still were the snake-handler sects that flourished in the southern United States during the same period and still exist today. Disciples believe that handling poisonous rattlesnakes demonstrates the intensity of their faith in divine protection. Police have not always extended freedom of worship to followers. Once, they raided a meeting in Virginia, where five thousand people had gathered. "When police charged," reported the *News Chronicle*, "the faith-healers swung the rattlesnakes over their heads, shouting: 'Come and get me. Praise the Lord.'"

"One touched his lips to the snake's fangs as he was being put into a police car. Another screamed and pulled a snake from beneath his shirt. It was clubbed to death."

CHAPTER SIX: THE WONDERS OF SCIENCE

Terrible Inventions

In Los Angeles, the city fathers once experimented with a device to make road accidents a pleasurable experience for victims. An upholstered plush couch was fixed to the front wheels of a tram, so that careless pedestrians would be scooped up in comfort. During a trial run, the luckless victim fell on the ground, not the couch, and was hurt. Then, torrential rain began to fall, soaking the upholstery—the project was abandoned.

Circular warships, theatres in whales, devices for appearing to be threelegged—what has not been invented?

A German inventor, Herr Krenkel, devised an ingenious life-saving suitcase into which victims of shipwrecks could climb while others drowned; he made much money out of it. A Belgian inventor named Vandertas devised a less successful "Fresh Air Machine" for poorly ventilated rooms. The ventilator consisted of a colossal metal megaphone covering half of the bed. People complained that the great black hole above them gave them nightmares from which they awoke to crack their heads on the rim.

Ingenious flying machines and passenger services were patented long before powered flight was a reality. The modern reader may smile, forgetting that America's Transworld Airlines applied for a license to fly passengers and mail to the moon as early as 1969. "We already have 5,000 bookings for lunar flights. Let's face it, someone is going to fly commercially to the moon at some time," said a spokesman.

But why sign up for a trip to the moon when a flight to Mars might not be that far off? In 2015, more than two hundred thousand people signed up for a one-way trip to Mars. As NASA and private companies worked to send inflatable living quarters to the red planet, other companies were already seeking to colonize the planet.

There is no way—at the moment—to return home to Earth, so a trip would be permanent. The interesting thing is the number of young fathers and mothers willing to leave their spouses and children behind in the name of space pioneerism.

One such person is Kellie Gerardi, who had just gotten engaged when she signed up for the trip. She told reporters that it would be hard to leave her future husband and possibly children but she wanted to be among the first to make the trip.

Much the same thought must have been in the minds of the entrepreneurs who advertised an aerial steam carriage in the *Illustrated London News* of 1842.

Some of the greatest inventors have wandered down the back alleyways of possibility. Thomas Edison, for example, invented a voice-driven sewing machine. The idea was to save the labor of pedaling by converting sound waves into power. Theoretically, there was nothing wrong with the device—and indeed it worked. The trouble was that users had to roar continuously into the mouthpiece—a much more exhausting procedure than merely pedaling.

Guglielmo Marconi, the pioneer of wireless telegraphy, claimed to have found a way of blowing up the most powerful battleships at a distance of some 20 miles (32 km) without using explosives of any description. All that was needed was that the enemy warship contain high explosives and be heavily coated with metal. The *Penny Pictorial* magazine of January 20, 1900, described Marconi's death waves as follows:

"His plan is this: He sets two spear-shaped wires on some high elevation, such as a turret or masthead. These are connected with a powerful dynamo fixed on the ground. So soon as the iron-clad is sighted the points of the wire arc."

New hopes for world nutrition were raised in 1977 when a research center in Copenhagen announced that it had successfully crossed tomato and potato plants. The "pomato," as the hybrid was termed, existed in the form of four fragile plants, said to be "doing well" in laboratory conditions. Unfortunately, the fruit of the resulting plant was deadly poisonous.

On the subject of unsaleable products for human consumption, mention should be made of a soft drink manufactured in Japan in the 1980s. Japanese drink manufacturers were seeking a product to vie with Coca-Cola. This version was known as Sweat.

According to the *New Scientist*, delicious refreshing Sweat came in cans that describe it as "a health orientated drink which supplies water and electrolytes lost through perspiration." The thirsty Japanese were assured that Sweat was "quickly absorbed into the body tissues due to its fine osmolality and ... is thus highly recommended as a beverage for such activities as sports, physical labor, after a hot bath, and even as an eye opener in the morning."

Some eye opener. And what does it taste like? According to the *New Scientist*: "In a word, and not to put too fine a point on it, like cold sweat."

After a can of Sweat, what could be more natural than to retire with a good book to the "smallest room" (bathroom) to contemplate in peace the infinite variety of human follies. For reading matter, bookbinders have come up with some quite remarkable products including a copy of the *Ancient Mariner* printed on seaweed and an edition or Wordsworth's *White Doe of Rylston* encased in "a simulated alligator skin and a cover that crumbles to dust in the hand." Discriminating readers may prefer an item with perhaps the most unsaleable title of all time: "*The Interpretation of Geological Time from the Evidence*

Close Encounter with a Spitting Cobra

The spitting cobra is one of the most terrifying reptiles in the animal kingdom. It directs a jet of venom into the eyes of its victim and can hit its target at a range of up to 6 feet (1.8 m). The poison is deadly for many creatures, and may cause blindness in humans. In November 1982, a Zimbabwe businessman named Kenneth Hampson had a perilous encounter with one such cobra and was saved by a mother's milk.

Hampson discovered the cobra in the engine of his car while travelling through the bush. As he reached under the hood to remove it, the creature spat into his eyes. Hampson staggered back, clutching at his face. Luckily, however, a man had stopped nearby in a truck. "He pushed me over to his wife, who was feeding a baby, and told her to squirt milk into my eyes," the businessman said. Hampson was then rushed to Bulawayo general hospital, where he was told that the woman's action had saved his sight.

Doctors explained that human milk is an excellent first aid remedy for cobra venom in the eyes. It neutralizes the neurotoxins present, diluting the poison and soothing the pain.

or Fossilised Elephant Droppings in Eastern Europe (translated from the Polish)."

Inside the smallest room, readers may be troubled by bright lights and mosquitoes and welcome a handy tip furnished by a correspondent of *Good Shopping*: "When my husband reads in bed on warm nights he puts a colander over his head. He says it keeps off the flies, shades his eyes from the light and lets in air at the same time."

Clearly there is an opening here for an imaginative entrepreneur to run a line in perforated nocturnal headgear. As for the smallest room itself, however, it seems that no further advances can be made. In September 1977, an American bidet company threatened the bathroom breakthrough of all time: a lavatory seat that washes and air-dries the crucial parts of the anatomy, rendering toilet paper unnecessary. The report, carried in the *Sunday Times*, was a little vague as to how the super toilet works in practice. Scalding jets of water? Mechanical hands? Suffice to say that it will save an average family of four fifty thousand sheets of toilet paper every year.

Paddling Icebergs to Arabia

In October 1977, Prince Mohammed al-Faisal, nephew of King Khalid of Saudi Arabia, flew a two-ton iceberg to the state of Iowa.

The prince's aim was to promote the "First International Conference on Iceberg Utilization," which was to take place during that month. And the prince also brought something else to Iowa—a vision of what the future might hold. For the prince was sustained above all by a fantastic plan to paddle icebergs from Antarctica to the desert wastes of Arabia, where their waters would be used to irrigate his country's arid and desolate zones.

The concept of iceberg utilization was not entirely new. During World War II, for example, some of the more wayward scientific advisers to the British government had suggested that man-made icebergs should be used as mid-Atlantic refueling stations. In the summer of 1977, a French company with its own plans for iceberg removal went bankrupt. The prince hit the headlines partly through his own fervent enthusiasm for his project and partly because the newfound wealth of the

Saudi Arabia's Prince Mohamed al-Faisal attempted to lobby for the study and utilization of icebergs in 1977.

Middle Eastern oil sheikhs seemed to make practically anything possible.

The Iowa iceberg conference, sponsored by the prince and reported in the *Times*, was attended by some two hundred respected scholars, attracted the interest of American science foundations and the US Coast Guard, as well as assorted entrepreneurs. The prince was quite aware of the obvious objections to his scheme, notably that the icebergs might melt by the time they reached the equator. But the operation was to be swift and efficient. The icebergs, he suggested, might be equipped "with their own propulsion system in the form of paddle wheels. Their power supply will originate from power generation units located either on top of the iceberg or provided from ships accompanying the iceberg."

As for the economics of the enterprise, the prince maintained that it all made sound financial sense. Desalination plants, for extracting fresh water from the sea, were immensely costly. In contrast, it was estimated that the cost of paddling a one hundred metric ton iceberg to Saudi Arabia would be a snap.

However, even supposing that shifting icebergs around the world was possible, there were serious legal and political problems to consider. A US State Department legal expert pointed out that several different countries had laid claim to parts of the Antarctic. Governments had not yet considered the legality of simply sailing south, catching an Antarctic iceberg, and towing it away. If the scheme really took off; a continent might be partially dismembered. The expert was interested in the prince's idea, but remained skeptical.

Of course, with today's fragile state of the polar icecaps and the problem of global warming, no one is going to be taking the icebergs anywhere. However, Anthony Mamo of Arlington Heights, Illinois, is the holder of patent number 4,320,989, covering a new method for iceberg propulsion over long distances.

Mamo, it transpired, had devised a method for moving icebergs through the oceans by using tiny air bubbles released through perforated tubes placed under one side of the iceberg. The movement of air should then propel the iceberg in the opposite direction. The inventor's patent suggests that the air could be pumped through tubes aboard one or more escort ships. No paddle wheels would be required; indeed, no contact with or boarding of the iceberg was necessary. Concluding, the *Telegraph* noted: "The inventor has successfully moved simulated icebergs in oceans."

Beware of Robots

More and more companies these days are relying on robots to do their work. But that's not all. The army has robot dogs, and some people are even buying companion robots. Haven't they seen any science fiction movies? Robots always try and take over, don't they?

A robot is an apparently human automaton; the term was coined as early as 1920, in a play called *R.U.R.* (Rossum's Universal Robots) written by the Czech writer Karel Čapek. *Robota* means "forced labor" in Czech, but since the machines have become a reality, safety advisers have had to draw up guides on how to keep robots subservient. In June 1982, the *Daily Telegraph* outlined some of the problems: "Unlike other automated machinery, robots move about in unpredictable patterns. Thus in a modern car works they look like malevolent ostriches, with necks and beaks making darting, stabbing actions as they wield welding equipment, spitting sparks."

Apprehensive *Guardian* readers were alarmed only two months later by a piece headlined: "Robot Jailed." It disclosed that a 4-foot (121-cm) robot was hauled off to jail when it was unable to give an account of itself as it strode, lights flashing, along the exclusive Beverly Drive in Los Angeles. A policeman was called to the scene, and when the robot failed to respond to questioning the suspect was taken to the station in a police van.

A police spokesman said: "The device was being operated by remote control, but the operator refused to come forward and identify himself—so the robot is spending the night in the station." He did not say whether the robot was being charged.

The potential of robots appears to be limitless. Already, the Japanese factory of Fanuc, 80 miles (128 km) west of Tokyo, is staffed by robots that make the parts for other robots. In this, the world's most advanced robot-manufacturing plant, up to a hundred robots are made each month. The factory runs twenty-four hours a day and has practically dispensed with human intervention. So far, the workforce seems content—there have been no strikes.

Will the robots eventually dispense with us altogether? The concept appears to belong to the realm of science fiction, and yet it is not as entirely fanciful as might be thought.

The advances made by AI, or artificial intelligence, over the years have been startling. Search engines use it to determine your likes, dislikes, and items on the Internet that interest you the most. They feed the data to their advertisers who then promptly fill your page with advertisements aimed specifically at you.

Newspaper websites are experimenting with doing the same thing in order to deliver a more tailored online newspaper for individual readers.

Of course, things can also get a little creepy. A recent segment on a television news station showed how one robotics/AI lab is running a "genetics" test on the machinery by placing the "brains," if you will, in boatlike devices designed to solve a puzzle while in a small pool. Only the devices that solve the riddles quickest are then used as processors for the next generation of robot. The robots are being developed by programmers known as "knowledge engineers." The ethical question—"Should it be allowed?"—is of no apparent concern.

The first "thinking" robots may have been the computers that were programmed to play the game of chess.

The First World Computer Chess Championship was held in Stockholm as early as 1974. Thirteen computers from eight countries took part: four from the United States, three from Britain, and one each from Austria, Canada, Hungary, Norway, Switzerland, and the USSR. As in many other international events, the competitors were seeded, with winners playing winners, losers playing losers and so on. The games were played out in four five-hour evening sessions. The top seed was a clever little number called 4.0 from Northwestern University, already the victor in several US computer chess championships.

The organizer of the contest, quoted in the *Sunday Times*, declared: "Computers are quite good at openings, which depend mainly on memory, and middle games. But they are very bad at end games. They often lose end games from a winning position. Overall, I would say computers are a bit above the level of the weaker club players."

In 2016, a Japanese company using both Japanese and Taiwanese technology could not keep its latest invention on the shelves. "Pepper" is a child-size companion robot and the first of its kind to understand and react to human emotions such as laughing or frowning. The newest model, which sold out in less than a minute after being made available online, is able to memorize using cloud technology.

An engineer puts finishing touches on a robotic dog. The dogs can help soldiers carry heavy equipment over challenging terrain.

It can also live autonomously at home while its owner or companion is at work and is supposed to have quite a sense of humor. Other companies have developed robotic dogs perfect for those who have allergies or just don't want to scoop poop.

The US military has also developed robotic dogs that are able to carry out battle commands, search for explosives, and carry gear for soldiers.

A Cabinet of Medical Curiosities

According to the *Charlotte Observer* in 1926, the Reverend Taylor and the Reverend Dick conducted a learned public debate at Edenton on the question: "Will the Negro retain his present color in heaven?" Taylor contended that the skin color of African Americans will indeed change.

It is not clear what scientific evidence Taylor marshalled to support his argument; the report merely illustrates how weirdly racial prejudice may affect otherwise intelligent people. But cases of individuals' skin changing color have occurred; and in places where racial laws operate, the results can be disquieting.

In January 1970 Alphons du Toit, for example, a South African white man, was stung from head to toe when he walked into a swarm of bees in the middle of Johannesburg. He turned black. A housewife was shopping nearby when the incident occurred, and declared: "He was unrecognizable." Another passerby telephoned for an ambulance. The official at the other end of the line asked: "European or non-European?" The passer-by replied; "Non-European—I think."

This occurred while South Africa was still living under apartheid rule and accordingly, du Toit was put into an ambulance for non-whites and driven to the non-white section of Johannesburg General Hospital for treatment. While the patient was being given emergency treatment, however, the nurses discovered that he was white. Should they carry on regardless? Or interrupt treatment to have du Toit moved to the white section? Prejudice won, and in a desperate state, the unfortunate patient was wheeled out of the non-white area and into the white. His condition was critical.

The vagaries of apartheid were further exposed by the case of Rita Hoefling, a white South African woman who had an operation to remove her adrenal glands in 1969. After the operation her skin turned progressively darker and darker, discolored by pituitary secretions. A Cape Town hospital worker, Hoefling found herself being treated as a black maid, ordered off whites-only buses, and subjected to countless slights and humiliations. In 1978 she wrote a formal letter to protest to the South African premier, John Vorster, to tell him "what apartheid is doing to my life and those of others."

The workings of the human body are strange indeed. Dora Watkinson trod on a darning needle one day, and part of it broke off and entered her foot. The foot was x-rayed and a fragment of the needle removed. She appeared to feel no ill effects. About a year later, however, her tongue started to scratch on something in her jaw—and she removed from between two of her lower teeth half an inch of the broken needle trodden on twelve months earlier. It had toured her body through the bloodstream.

One curious case, and distressing no doubt, was that of twelve-year-old Tricia Reay. The young girl simply could not stop sneezing. On March 19, 1980, the newspapers announced that she had scored a world record for Britain by sneezing non-stop for 156 days, and still she kept on sneezing, on average, once every twenty seconds. Relief was to come eventually when she was taken from her home to a specialized clinic where doctors managed to cure the condition. When the sneezing finally stopped, Tricia had sneezed for over two hundred days!

One Florida teen had a similar malady except her affliction was a neverending case of the hiccups.

In 2010, then fifteen-year-old Jennifer Mee was thrust into the national spotlight when she could simply not stop hiccupping. She appeared on just about every popular news show and was given a ton of support. She tried home remedies, acupuncture, and even hypnotism, in addition to traditional medical treatment.

Nothing seemed to work until one day, out of the blue, the hiccups just stopped on their own.

Unfortunately for Mee, who was also said to suffer from Tourette's syndrome and schizophrenia, this was not the last time we would hear her name on the news.

In 2013, at the age of twenty-two, Mee was convicted of first degree murder and sentenced to life in prison for her part in a drug deal gone bad. While Mee did not take part in the murder of the victim, she orchestrated the robbery.

While various nations around the world sought a cure for the common cold, South Africa devoted its attention to developing a device that would *cause* people to sneeze. The Sneeze Machine was developed as an aid to riot control, and sprayed crowds with a mixture of talcum powder and tear gas. It made its first appearance in 1977. Opponents of South Africa's apartheid regime derived some comfort only two weeks later when newspapers reported that the police officer who operated the device was himself in hospital in Johannesburg—suffering from tear-gas poisoning. He had been overexposed to the talc and tears mixture while using the machine on black students in Soweto.

Home cures for commonplace ailments have been colorfully reported over the years. One of the most persistent pieces of advice is to get stung by a bee as a cure for rheumatism; if it really works, it is because the formic acid present in bee venom acts as a counterirritant. Of less certain efficiency are such remedies as boiled cockroaches stuffed into a bad ear and infusions of mice applied to a bad back. During a whooping cough epidemic of 1892, the *Times* recalled that Charlotte M. Yonge, a Victorian novelist, made the choice "to be taken to the top of a steep place, then violently pushed down," and "to have gunpowder in bags round the wrists set on fire."

By the year 2000 the black market for human organs jumped off the pages of a sci-fi novel to real life. The sordid story came to light after it was discovered that organ traders were exploiting some of the poorest people in the world—those living in Brazil's worst and largest slum. The traders were approaching unsuspecting, uneducated, and desperately poor people offering large sums of money for their organs.

One man told the *New York Times* he had sold his kidney for $6,000, more money than he had ever seen in his life. He is already suffering health complications from his decision.

Thousands of others—also in desperate situations—have come forward offering their organs and body parts for money.

For sheer Gothic horror, however, the following snippet surely surpasses all. It has caused at least one researcher (the author) to shriek aloud in the silence of the Bodleian Library in Oxford, England. You have been warned:

"Paris—The former director of the French eye bank, has been charged with manslaughter after the death of a man who was given the cornea of a rabies victim during an eye operation. The eye bank was later closed."

Crash Tests—Macabre Experiments

Before air bags were commonplace lifesavers in automobiles, the companies that devised them had to run rigorous tests , and not all of them used crash test dummies.

Some grim and controversial experiments conducted in Germany played their part in air bag development. Fresh corpses were crashed against walls by scientists examining the air bags' effectiveness.

The story hit the headlines in December 1970. At that time, it was widely believed that the inflatable safety bags

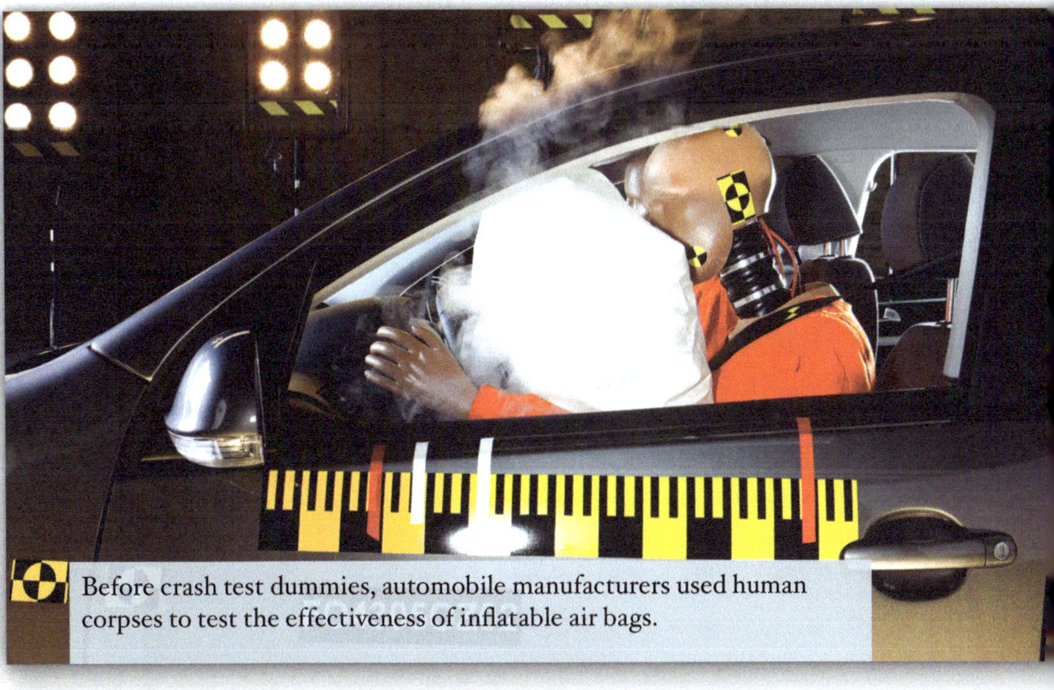

Before crash test dummies, automobile manufacturers used human corpses to test the effectiveness of inflatable air bags.

would become required wearing in the United States within three years. Car manufacturers in North America and Europe opposed the devices on the grounds that they were too expensive and that their efficiency was suspect.

Experiments had, of course, been performed with dummies—but dummies did not behave exactly like living bodies. You could not crash normal healthy people against walls for obvious reasons, and the next best things were corpses. An American university tried experiments with dead bodies, but they had to use corpses that were up to six months old. The peculiarly macabre aspect of the German experiments was that the bodies were those of people who had just died—they had practically been whisked from the undertakers' slabs, strapped into vehicles, and sent careening off to a second death.

The experiments had been conducted in secret by a medical institute working with leading motor safety engineers. A highly respected passenger car development engineer described the air bags' hazards to a *Times* reporter: "We have theoretically killed people with the air bag. Sometimes it has come up the right way; or knocked against his chin; or knocked his head back and broken his neck. With dummies you would get readings of the force exerted but you would not know what happened to his neck. It is not exactly the same. You have to have movable bodies which are no more than three hours dead."

The corpses, the engineer explained, were unidentified bodies and those given before death for medical research. In Britain, a film of the macabre "experiments" was to have been shown to a group of engineers in the Midlands, but it was decided that the screening of jolting and lurching corpses would be "too gruesome."

A similar controversy raged in the United States early in 1978. In this case, however, the victims of the crash tests were live.

"Save the Baboon Seven!" the car stickers flashed from bumpers and back windscreens throughout the streets of Detroit in February of that year. The baboons in question were seven innocent African baboons scheduled to be slaughtered in the interests of science. Once again, experiments for passenger safety were at the heart of the furor. The baboons were to be anaesthetized and strapped onto impact sleds that would hurtle them into an object which would inflict severe chest injury. The injured animal would them be examined and "terminated" before they regained consciousness.

The tests were to be conducted by the University of Michigan in Ann Arbor. Officials at the Highway Research Institute there explained that the study was aimed at developing lifelike dummies that would eliminate the need for using animals or human corpses in future crash tests. The project director was puzzled why the baboons' fate should outrage public opinion. Similar tests had been carried out since 1974 at various universities around the United States. Twenty-three baboons, shipped from Africa, it was learned, had already met their deaths in the experiments; dummies, computer models, and human corpses had also been used. "This is the first time anything like this has come up," the director told reporters.

Heading the Save the Baboon Seven Committee was a Unitarian minister, who said: "It is frightening and appalling to think that people would treat animals in this way, particularly at a time of rising consciousness and concern over conservation; it flies in the face of decency and concern for living things." And he was not alone in his sense of outrage.

The campaign to save the doomed baboons captured the public imagination as few efforts by antivivisectionists had done before. Perhaps it was the surreal quality of the proposed experiments that did the trick—it was not hard for human beings to identify with monkeys strapped powerless into vehicles and propelled towards certain death, while the fates of guinea pigs in obscure laboratories could be conveniently ignored. In all events, the campaign was a partial success.

One of the seven was sacrificed to science, but the six remaining baboons earned a reprieve. Later, scientists at the University of Michigan declared that they had enough data from earlier experiments to complete their study—without further tests on baboons.

CLONING AND THE CARBON COPY MAN

The development of cloning techniques received little press attention at the outset. And yet it carried such weird implications that it is surprising that they were not grasped immediately.

Cloning is a method of producing perfect living copies of plants or animals, by transplanting a cell nucleus from an adult into an embryonic environment. Gardeners had, in fact, been practicing a form of cloning for centuries by taking cuttings from one plant to establish another—bypassing the natural process of seeding. The cells of adult animals, and humans too, contain the same genetic information as the embryo. So it ought to be possible to "take cuttings" in the form of a cell nucleus and nurture a duplicate being in the ovum.

This is precisely what happened during the 1970s, when scientists managed on several occasions to produce clone frogs. Cells from living frogs were implanted in frog ova—frogspawn—from which the existing embryo cells had been removed. Frogs identical to the cell "parent" were created.

Then came the sensation.

In 1978, science journalist David M. Rorvik published a book claiming that he had helped a millionaire to produce a clone offspring—a carbon copy of himself. The book, *In His Own Image*, became the centerpiece of a public and scientific furor. Briefly told, Rorvik's story was that he had helped the millionaire find a gynecologist who was sufficiently skilled—

and willing—to carry out the procedure. To carry the scheme through, the gynecologist had gone to a developing nation with a plentiful supply of women willing to undergo experimental pregnancies. The book asserted that the technique had worked; a child had been born and was now two years old.

Since neither the millionaire nor the gynecologist were named, the story suggested a hoax. Scientists pointed out that though frogs had certainly been cloned, no authenticated case of a duplicated mammal existed—not even a mouse. A mammal was an immensely more complex creature and a human being more complex still. The technology simply was not there. Test-tube babies were not yet a reality, and cloning a child was a far more daunting task than test-tube fertilization.

And yet, in a curious way, it did not seem to matter very much whether Rorvik's book was fact or fiction. For the first time it presented before the general public the possibility that human cloning was within the reach of modern science. Might a genius be cloned? Or a Hitler? (Ira Levin made the latter possibility the theme of a best-selling novel, *The Boys from Brazil*.)

In general, scientists agreed that cloning human beings was a theatrical possibility—but that true carbon copies presented insurmountable problems. The human ovum was very different from frogspawn. Cells introduced into it would be affected by "foreign" proteins, influencing the development of the embryo with their own genetic characteristics. In the journal *Science*, a contributor pointed out that to stand a chance of creating a true duplicate, an individual would have to transplant a cell nucleus into an ovum taken from his or her own mother.

And quite apart from the biological complexities, the whole issue ignored the influence of the environment on shaping an individual's character and attributes.

Yet for all the skepticism of the scientists, the possibility of human cloning had been established in the public mind, and it left disquieting ethical problems to be faced.

As a footnote to the case of the carbon copy man, it is worth pointing out that a "cell zoo" already exists in the United States, in a Houston hospital. In this twentieth century Noah's Ark, animals from aardvarks to zebras are being preserved at a temperature of -310°F (-190° C). The animals are represented by cell samples taken from their skin, cultured, grown, and frozen. Threatened species such as exotic bats and a white rhinoceros are collected with special care. It is anticipated that the cells will survive for a thousand years—giving ample time for scientists to develop cloning to the point where it is possible to bring extinct species back from their cells alone. And if it's good enough for zebras ...

The Nobel Sperm Bank

Test-tube babies, artificial insemination—the advances of modern medicine have throughout history created bizarre legal and ethical dilemmas which perplex scientists and lawyers as much as the general public. Should pop stars be allowed to market their sperm commercially? Or Olympic athletes? Grotesque as the concepts appear, they were raised in a very real fashion in 1980, when the newspapers announced the opening of a repository that became known as the Nobel Sperm Bank.

Like so many of the world's weirdest developments, the idea dawned in California. The *Los Angeles Times* broke the story: three exceptionally intelligent women, it alleged, had been fertilized from a sperm bank that accepted only Nobel Prize winners as donors. The babies due that year would be the first to result from a scheme devised by a California millionaire named Robert Graham, inventor of plastic eyeglass lenses. The aim, said the newspaper, was to produce people of a superior intelligence.

One of the donors was William Shockley, aged seventy. Shockley had shared the Nobel Prize for Physics in 1956 and confirmed his participation in the program: "Yes, I'm one of them," he told reporters, and went on to express disappointment that more of his fellow Nobel scientists had not been prepared to contribute to "this good cause." Four other prizewinners had, nevertheless, taken part in the experiment. Robert Graham was quoted as saying that of the five donors, three had provided repeated samples. Their sperm was stored in an underground chamber lined with lead to protect it against radiation.

Unlike existing sperm banks, Graham's repository offered a good deal of information about the donors. Male participants filled out forms giving such details as their height, weight, and many other characteristics. Only their names were withheld. Apart from the three women fertilized, it was claimed, more than a dozen had expressed interest in the idea.

The immediate public reaction was one of profound disquiet. The repository seemed to evoke Hitlerian ambitions of creating a master race, an elite of geniuses. However, Robert Graham told reporters: "I don't see any parallel. We are not thinking of a super race; we are thinking in terms of a few more creative intelligent people who otherwise would not be born." In fact, he went farther, cheerfully expressing the hope that sperm banks would be established for "Olympic gold medalists, artists, or movie stars."

In general, scientists were deeply skeptical about the whole program. Leaving ethical issues aside, there was no evidence to suggest in any field—be it science, entertainment, or the arts—that genius "ran in the family" genetically. Obviously, famous families of, for example, violinists, did exist, but the proficiency of members was more likely to stem from enthusiasm, in the home environment than from heredity.

One Nobel Prize winner commented: "I think it's pretty silly." Another said, "What surprises me is that any woman would want this. But I guess people are entitled to do what they want."

The *Los Angeles Times* contacted twenty-three Nobel scientists when the story first broke. Eleven said that they had been approached by Graham, and all except Shockley said that they had refused.

In fact, since its initiation, the Nobel Sperm Bank (or Repository for Germinal Choice, as it is officially termed) has been forced to lower its sights as far as donors are concerned. Too few Nobel Prize winners have been prepared to contribute samples. Some have objected to the ethics of the project, others to the notions of heredity on which it is based. In a few cases, prize winners have been too old for their sperm to be fertile.

The repository was a failure and was closed in 1999. As for the babies themselves, fathered from the lead-lined concrete bunker, fifteen were born.

The birth of the first child, Victoria, revived the controversy. The child was born in April 1982 to a housewife, thirty-nine, of Phoenix, Arizona. The delivery itself went very well, but some awkward discoveries were made about the mother and her second husband. To begin with, they had both served sentences for mail fraud by using the records of dead children and others to get credit card and bank loans. But more was to come.

It emerged that the couple had lost custody of the mother's two children by her first marriage—after both children were subjected to bizarre abuse in attempts to get them "to do work and be smart."

State investigators discovered that their stepfather beat the children with straps, forced them to sleep in the kitchen and on the living room floor, and humiliated them publicly. Interviewed by the *Washington Post*, the youngsters confirmed the stories. Both said that the couple gave them considerable amounts of extra homework and punished them if they made mistakes. They said that Eric, the boy, was once forced to go to school in his pajamas and slippers wearing a sign saying that he was a bed wetter.

Donna, the girl, was sometimes made to wear a sign on her forehead reading "dummy."

Robert Graham was defensive about the birth and future of his first "superbaby." Speaking of the mother, he said, "She did produce a superb infant, as good as they come. We can't hope to be 100 percent perfect in our selection." However, the sperm bank now required potential mothers to fill in a detailed twenty-page questionnaire in an attempt to improve the "screening" of parents.

CHAPTER SEVEN: PHENOMENA

STRANGE NATURE

Breakfast was a colorful occasion for retirees Jim and Lillian Harbery. Their hen Goldie laid blue eggs. "When she laid her first blue egg I didn't really think a great deal about it," Mrs. Harbery told reporters at her home in Cornwall. "But when she laid six in a row it shook me a bit."

Stranger still was the case or a hen belonging to Jack Pelter. His hen laid perfectly normal eggs for two years—and then turned into a rooster.

From the earliest days of the press, newspapers have delighted in reporting curious natural phenomena, be they sex-change hens or six-legged calves. Among such freaks of nature, the following item is hard to beat for silent menace: "An eighteen-inch snake, with two heads and two tails, was captured in the town of Saladillo today. One head eats voraciously, but the other does not function at all." (*Times*, May 14, 1975)

For sheer weirdness, however, the widely reported cat with wings, found in an Oxford garden in 1933, surpasses all. "I have just seen a cat that has on its back fully-developed fur-covered wings, with which, it is stated, it can fly," announced an incredulous reporter. The bizarre creature had been found by an Oxford housewife. With black-and-white markings, the feline freak was prowling around her back garden; later it found its way into her stables. "I saw it move from the ground to a beam—a considerable distance, which I do not think it could have leaped using its wings in a manner similar to that of a bird," she said.

Two officials arrived from the Oxford Zoo and captured the animal, which was placed on display in the zoo. "I carefully examined the cat tonight," a reporter declared, "and there is no doubt about the wings. They grow just in front of its hindquarters."

Some creatures are born strange; others acquire strangeness through circumstances. "Mice Grow Fur Wraps in Freezer," announced the *Daily Telegraph* on July 15, 1982, and it had a curious tale to tell. In Norwich, England, a family of mice had found their way into a refrigerated room stocked with frozen meat carcasses. The conditions were arctic, with temperatures maintained at between -14 and - 18°F (- 26 and - 28 °C). The mice survived by growing extra-thick woolly coats. A health official said: "They were just like little balls of fluff and looked quite different from ordinary mice. It must have taken them several months to adapt to the conditions but it shows how quickly they can change to suit their environment."

The super mice lived on rock-hard frozen meat carcasses in the refrigerated room until they were rounded up by astonished pest control experts. The official continued: "Half a dozen of these fluffy mice were caught and I was amazed when I saw them. It certainly is the most unusual case of survivors that I have ever come across. They were completely immune to commonly used rat poison. When they were fed with it they thrived." How they got in remained somewhat mysterious, but it was pointed out that it was almost impossible to make anywhere totally mouse-proof: "They can squeeze through a gap only an eighth of an inch wide by flattening their skulls."

The flexibility of mice, however, pales to insignificance beside the discovery made by biologists at Michigan State University in 1977. Their research showed that headless cockroaches learn quicker than their intact counterparts. The *Sunday Times*, reporting this curious phenomenon, announced that "headless cockroaches can live for seven days after beheadings because of nerve cell clusters elsewhere in their bodies. The Michigan researchers report that the roaches learn to avoid painful electric shocks more quickly than normal ones with heads."

A little on the cuter side, scientists in 2010 announced the discovery of a new species of monkey called the snubnose monkey discovered in the Himalayan mountains. The little creatures have upside down noses, or rather, noses that face upwards. The only problem is that when it rains the monkeys collect rainwater in their noses and can't help but start sneezing over and over. They have been dubbed the sneezing monkeys. But, they have learned to cope with this curious phenomenon: the monkeys have been observed with their little heads tucked in between their knees during rain showers in order to keep their inner nostrils dry.

The snubnose monkey's upside-down nose adds to the animal's appeal, but it is no help during rainstorms.

The private life of plants is imbued with mystery. Experiments conducted with polygraphs (lie detectors) suggest that vegetation responds to threat or caress much as plant lovers have asserted for generations. The case of Norfolk's Weeping Tree, however, took plant sensitivity beyond the bounds of normal expectation. The tree, at Stonehouse Farm, West Harling, began crying in 1939. Tears trickled incessantly down trunk and branches in perfectly dry weather. When puzzled villagers cut away a branch, tears positively gushed from the wound. Examined by experts, the phenomena finally submitted to an orthodox explanation: an underground spring had forced its way up through the trunk.

THE ELECTRIC MAN

The spoon-bending feats of Uri Geller and other mentalists are celebrated throughout the world. And yet otherwise ordinary people with weird electric talents have been reported on several occasions, their achievements predating Geller's by many years.

Take the case of Charles Borkett, reported in the *Daily Mirror* in 1952: "When Mrs. Borkett wakes up in the early morning and sees violet sparks flying in the darkness, she doesn't scream—she knows it is her husband Charles rubbing a 'dud' electric bulb to get sufficient light to see the bedside clock. It's easier than putting on the light." Charles Borkett, aged sixty-three, could take a bulb with a broken filament, rub it smartly, and then, by stroking it with long, slender fingers, produce a bright violet flash inside the glass. He demonstrated his powers to reporters at his home in Port Talbot. Three bulbs—two with broken filaments and one intact—glowed with the weird violet light as he handled them.

An Aerial Steam Carriage

This is the name that has been given to a new machine, for which a company has taken out a patent and which is to convey passengers, goods, and dispatches through the air, performing the journey from London to India in four days and to travel at the rate of seventy-five to one hundred miles per hour. Absurd and chimerical as this scheme appears, we understand that a company has been really formed to carry it into operation, and that the patent was formally sealed on the 29th of September last. In January the machine will be thoroughly organized, and until then we take leave of the subject, and only trust that this alleged invention is neither exaggerated nor an Utopian project.

—*Illustrated London News*, **November 12, 1842**

A former railway signalman, Borkett first discovered his talent when his bicycle light failed on the way to work. He told reporters: "I know quite a bit about electricity, but I can't explain this. Glass is an insulator, yet it seems that electricity is being transmitted from my body through the glass to create light inside the bulb."

An electrical engineer commented: "This man probably has exceptionally dry skin, and if he applied a little friction to the glass of the bulbs, it would be sufficient to create light inside the bulb."

The Lady with Broadcaster's Teeth

Among all the bizarre maladies that may afflict a human being, the prize for weird comedy must surely be awarded to the broadcaster's teeth possessed by a housewife of Daytona Beach, Florida.

The lady in question agreed to talk to reporters only if her name was withheld; the phenomenon was an acute embarrassment to her. For the purposes of this piece we will call her Mrs. X—but should incredulous readers doubt the account, they may confirm it by consulting the *Ottawa Journal* of April 9, 1970.

Mrs. X began to receive musical radio signals through her teeth one night in 1970. Whenever she opened her mouth, her teeth transmitted songs that included "A Long Way to Tipperary" and "Rambling Rose."

Understandably distressed, Mrs. X sought medical advice.

Electronics experts declared that the music was played by someone using a wireless phonograph to send signals from one part of his or her house to another. A dentist explained why Mrs. X's teeth were picking up the signals. It appeared that fillings made up of two metals such as gold and amalgam could combine with the acid in human saliva to set up a receiving system—Mrs. X's mouth. The housewife placed an advertisement in a local newspaper urging whoever had been playing the songs to identify himself. A flood of calls ensued, "but nothing concrete."

The exhausted Mrs. X then moved out of her neighborhood and took to sleeping in a motel, out of range of the wireless enthusiast, to get some peace. But this offered no long-term solution. Finally, Mrs. X became desperate. One Wednesday in April she had all her fillings but one replaced by plastic. The remaining metal filling was left because it involved a root and might have to be pulled.

The music stopped for three days. "I thought I was free and was ready to throw a party," she said.

And then her teeth tuned up again. "Rambling Rose, Rambling Rose." The music was much weaker than before, but still present, humming away in the last metallic molar.

Mystery File

The Loch Ness monster saga really began with a now famous report of May 2, 1933, carried in the Inverness [Scotland] *Courier*. "Strange Spectacle on Loch Ness" announced the headline, and the article went on to describe how an Inverness businessman and his wife had seen a creature which "disported itself, rolling and plunging for fully a minute, its body resembling that of a whale, and the water cascading and churning like a simmering cauldron."

In fact, Nessie had been sighted as early as 565 BCE by an Irish monk. The *Times* in 1856 had reported a "Sea Serpent in the Highlands." But it was only after the Inverness couple's sighting that the monster became a popular obsession. Photographs were published, new sightings made—throughout the summer of 1933, the press had a field day. The story has never quite died. Though perhaps some of the mystery has. Over the years there had been speculation that the "monster" was indeed nothing more than a giant Wells catfish or a Greenland shark as theorized by fisherman and television personality Jeremy Wade in 2013.

But in 1994, Christian Spurling made a startling deathbed confession. The famous 1934 photos had been part of an elaborate hoax and kept a family secret for years. The funny thing is that despite the admission of fraud, there are many who still believe the monster is real and lurking in the deepest part of the lake.

The Abominable Snowman earned his name in 1920. Like Nessie, he was the subject of legends and reports dating to a much earlier period. However, it was after the first British Mount Everest expedition sighted elusive figures that left huge footprints at about 17,000 feet (5,181 m) that the press really got its teeth into the story. The Sherpa guides identified the creatures under various locally used names—one of which was mistranslated as "Abominable Snowman."

Who were the hairy humanoids that trod the Himalayan snows? Footprints were photographed in 1937. Controversy raged in the press. Were they left by Neanderthals? Human outcasts? Brown bears? The most curious piece of evidence produced was a yeti scalp, of which a photographed appeared in the *London News* in 1954. It was supplied by a Professor C. von Fiirer-Haimendorf, a noted anthropologist. The professor had discovered the scalp among various ritual objects kept in a small Buddhist temple at Pangboche village. Even he doubted that it was a true scalp, however, claiming instead that it was probably "a piece of hide from another part of the body, molded into its present shape while still fresh and pliable." The article was made of tough skin, with sparse, bristly hair of brownish color. It was later discovered that three such scalps existed.

Sherpas declared yetis to be common sights and generally harmless. As late as 1974, however, the *Sunday Times* reported that a nineteen-year-old yak herder had been assaulted by a 4-foot (121-cm) yeti, which attacked her herd and killed five by twisting their horns. Nepalese police had "confirmed" the attack, and a photographer had recorded the footprints.

The infamous monster known as the "Chupacabra" or "Goatsucker" has plagued many farmers in Latin countries.

The first reports of the Chupacabra are from 1995 in Puerto Rico, where a creature was said to be sucking the blood of livestock, especially goats. Since then the upright, alien-like creature has been "spotted" as far north as Maine and as far south as Chile in South America. It has even made it to Europe and Asia.

No one has definitively proved what is or isn't the Chupacabra but one thing is certain, animals are being drained of their blood. The theory that most share, especially in the United States where rangers and farmers have shot and killed several suspected "Chupacabras," is that they are coyote-dog hybrids that are sick with mange and parasites that give them a very disturbing and even horrific appearance.

This problem has proved the most daunting to serious investigators of the UFO phenomenon. It is not hard to set up a plausible hoax, while it is an immensely difficult task to expose it. Strange objects have been reported in the skies since the beginning of written history, and unidentified flying objects were copiously reported in the nineteenth-century newspapers, but it was only when the press found a catchy tag for them that the reports really began to flood in.

It happened in June 1947, when American pilot Kenneth Arnold described sighting a formation of luminous objects "that flew like a saucer would if you skipped it across the water." The press called them flying saucers, and a new popular obsession was born.

It would be impossible to catalog here all the bizarre craft that have been sighted, photographed, and sometimes apparently tracked on radar screens. Occupants have come in all shapes and sizes, from little green men to the "Silver Giant from Outer Space" reported by a Manchester engineer in March 1978 (it was 7 feet (213 cm) tall, with "two pencil light-beams coming from eye-level"). Wildly improbable as many accounts of alien encounters and kidnappings have been, a few cases remain authentically mysterious.

To take a single example from the *Times* in 1978:

A full scale search has resumed today for a single-engined Cessna 182 which disappeared over the Bass Strait seven minutes after the pilot, Frederick Valentich, aged twenty, reported sighting an unidentified object on Saturday. Valentich, on his way to King Island from Melbourne, reported seeing a long object with a "green light and [its] sort of metallic like."

The pilot, the article continued, had been alone in the aircraft, and informed ground control at Melbourne that he was being followed by a large aircraft with four bright lights. It was travelling at high speed.

Just after 7 p.m., the controllers asked the pilot whether he could identify the aircraft. Valentich replied: "It's not an aircraft, It's ..."

The transmission ceased. Two minutes later, however, it resumed with the pilot announcing: "I'm orbiting and the thing is orbiting on top of me also ... it has a green light and [is] sort of metallic like on the outside."

Then the pilot reported that his engine was choking and rough-idling, and the object was hovering over him. There was noise in the transmission and contact with the aircraft was lost.

Valentich was never seen again.

Two Horrible Blobs

Conventional monsters such as Nessie and the yeti at least have something to recommend them; even the wildest reports credit them with some recognizable features, be they the attributes of dinosaur or ape.

More nightmarish, more abominable were two hideous, shapeless blobs cast up on the shore in the early 1960s. In March 1962, the *Daily Telegraph* reported that the body of a giant sea monster had been washed up on the desolate Tasmanian coast. The creature baffled scientists, having no defined head, eyes, or other sense organs.

The hulking brute was 20 feet (6 m) long and 18 feet (5 m) wide, and its estimated live weight was about eight tons. Though the body was in an advanced state of decomposition, "the flesh was extremely tough, like glass fiber." A party of scientists reported that it had a frill and gill-like slits and believed that the creature was "definitely not a mammal."

No less alarming was the "huge, shapeless mass of flesh and hair" that appeared on the sand at Muriwai Beach near Auckland in New Zealand, in 1965. Australia's *Townsville Bulletin* commented: "The thing was first sighted a week ago by a marine department officer. Then the hairy blob of flesh was thirty feet long and eight feet high. It is slowly being swallowed by the sand but more than twenty feet of it was still showing yesterday."

The head of Auckland's university zoology department said: "You can rule out whales because of the hair, and you can rule out sea elephants and sea cows because of its size."

How did it live, this creature? How did it breathe? The object was encased in a tough, quarter-inch thick hide. Below was a layer of fat, and beneath it, the scientists determined, was something fleshy.

Invasion of the blobs? Deep are the mysteries of the ocean. However, readers of delicate temperament will be relieved to know that in both these cases, scientists later revealed the carcasses to be decomposing masses of whale blubber.

And while the elusive giant squid was long to be thought a fiction dreamt up by Jules Verne, the long, nasty scars on the equally elusive sperm whales have proved that the epic battles between whale and giant squid do indeed take place thousands of feet below the water's surface.

THE MINNESOTA ICEMAN

Bernard Heuvelmans, an eminent Belgian zoologist, had researched and written about many rare creatures during his long and distinguished career. He had studied reports on the Himalayan yeti, publishing his conclusions in *On the Track of Unknown Animals*. He had made it a rule never to reject out-of-hand even the wildest rumors concerning strange animals. For Heuvelmans had found that even the most improbable tales might have some foundation in truth.

The case of the Minnesota Iceman, however, beat them all.

"Is it a Fake? Is it an Ape? or is it ... Neanderthal Man?" asked the headline of an extended feature in the *Sunday Times* of March 23, 1969, from which much of the following information is drawn: "A strange ape-like creature frozen in a block of ice is providing American anthropologists with one of the most intriguing questions they have faced in recent years. Is it a fraud, a freak, or is it a form of human being believed to have been extinct since prehistoric times? One thing is certain; it has two large bulletholes in it. Just as a precaution, the FBI have been called in."

Is it real or fake? Ivan T. Sanderson (above, with the "Minnesota Iceman") invited zoologist Bernard Heuvelmans to examine the ice-encased Neanderthal.

Heuvelmans had been invited to view the creature in New Jersey by science writer Ivan Sanderson. Imprisoned in its frozen coffin, the iceman was in the custody of a Minnesotan showman called Frank Hansen. Hansen said that it had been found floating in a block of ice in the Bering Strait and had been purchased in Hong Kong.

Hansen believed that the creature had existed for centuries in the ice block. This was unlikely. Heuvelmans knew that even if a living creature is frozen in natural ice at death it will start decaying very rapidly: Siberia's frozen mammoths were preserved in bog ice, which has antiseptic properties. But as the expert examined the showman's exhibit in an ill-lit trailer, he grew more and more excited. Using a flashlight to illuminate the creature, he listed its salient features.

The Iceman was 6 feet (182 cm) tall and covered all over with brown hair. The skin appeared white and waxlike. The neck was short and the torso barrel-shaped. Long arms terminated in huge hands.

One arm was bent at a peculiar angle, apparently broken. There was a gaping hole in the left eye. Examining the creature through the clouded ice, Heuvelmans concluded that it had been shot fairly recently with a high-caliber rifle. One bullet had passed through the arm, which it may have raised to protect itself; the other had penetrated the eye. The expert was unable to examine the back of the head, but Hansen stated that it had been shattered.

The feet were not those of ape or man. The big toe was unable to move freely like a thumb and this suggested an ape. But the soles of the feet were too wrinkled. The soles, moreover, were more markedly padded than those of a human being.

Systematically, Heuvelmans drew up a list of possibilities: was it a manufactured fake? This seemed improbable. A hoaxer would have had to reproduce the hair in incredibly minute detail. The ice, moreover, had been scraped away in parts to give people a closer look. In one place it had been pared off so much that the expert could smell decaying flesh. Heuvelmans dismissed the possibility of the thing being fashioned from plastic or wax.

Was it a composite creature, stitched together out of the limbs of different animals? Certainly there were precedents for such an exhibit. In the nineteenth century, for example, fake mermaids were commonly created by fitting together the top halves of monkeys and the bottom halves of fish. But to create the Iceman, the faker would have needed a hairy human head and the body and limbs of a gigantic ape, and where might the extraordinary feet be obtained?

Was it the corpse of some freakish human being? This theory stretched the bounds of credulity. Even the most bizarre fairground curiosities could not compete with the Iceman for deformity.

Was it then some unknown species of *Homo sapiens*, even a surviving Neanderthal man? Neanderthals were a species of early man that existed before *Homo sapiens* evolved. The Iceman had the long arms, short neck, barrel chest, and large hands and feet associated with early hominids. The feet, with their long second and third digits, were especially reminiscent of what was known of Neanderthals.

Incredible as the proposition appeared, Heuvelmans found himself tormented. For many nights after he viewed the exhibit he could not sleep. Since the creature had clearly been shot in recent years, it seemed to reinforce theories than a race of unknown hominids existed in the remoter parts of Asia.

The expert was anxious to buy the Iceman, but Hansen was reluctant to part with it. Heuvelmans turned to the Smithsonian Institution in Washington, which took an immediate interest and an investigating team was set up. Heuvelmans, meanwhile, published his findings in Belgium, provoking intense enthusiasm among his colleagues. Also interested were the FBI—for if something like a human being had been shot and killed, a capital crime might have been committed.

It seemed that the anthropological world was on the verge of one of the most exciting discoveries ever made in the study of man. And then, a veil of mystery descended over the affair.

Frank Hansen claimed that the Iceman was the property of a wealthy, unidentified man. The owner took possession of it, and only allowed a replica to be exhibited in future. The Smithsonian Institution was allowed to see the model—but not the original. They concluded that a hoax was being perpetrated while the FBI declared that there was not enough evidence for them to proceed, either.

Hansen, meanwhile, took an exhibit (it was not clear whether it was the original or the replica) to Canada to show at provincial fairs. On the way back to the United States, customs officials seized it. They stated that Hansen did not have the proper documentation to return a "hominid" to the country. The showman described it as a "fabricated illusion"; the customs officials asked to see core samples.

Hansen refused, on the grounds that removing samples would ruin his exhibit. Eventually, after telephoning his senator and a lawyer, he managed to get the creature back to the United States without an investigation and continued to show the Iceman at carnivals for some months. But the showman alleged that his contract to display the object ran out in the spring of 1970. Thereafter, the owner took possession, and the exhibit was withdrawn from public view.

The lack of positive evidence has made most zoologists conclude that the Iceman must have been a clever fake. Heuvelmans, however, remains convinced that there was something more to the frozen creature he examined in the torch-lit trailer. An aura of mystery lingered about the whole affair until the Iceman mysteriously resurfaced in 2013. This time, the creature was on eBay, the online auction site.

The eBay listing read: "This is the actual sideshow gaff billed as 'The Minnesota Iceman' by Frank Hansen in the 1960s. This is a one of a kind hoax that was fabricated by a mid-twentieth century showman."

The buyer was a Texas man who owned the Museum of the Weird.

THEY CAME FROM THE SKY!

All kinds of bizarre objects have been purported to drop from the sky, from monster hailstones to blocks of frozen urine. But the most remarkable falls have concerned living creatures—fish, frogs, and even worms. They have been so commonly reported, in fact, that they have scarcely been deemed worthy of more than a snippet in newspapers. The *Scientific American* of July 12, 1873, for example, noted: "A shower of frogs which darkened the air and covered the ground for a long distance is the reported result of a recent rainstorm in Kansas City, MO." A North African event drew an even terser statement from the *Sunday Times* of December 18, 1977: "It was raining frogs in the Moroccan Sahara last week. Freak whirlwinds are blamed."

Those "freak whirlwinds" have commonly been blamed for fishfalls too. Slithering cascades were reported in Singapore in 1861, following an earthquake: torrents of fish fell in the streets and were collected by the bucketful. Skeptics believed that the fish had in fact issued from the flood waters of swollen rivers, but one reporter found fish in his own walled courtyard which the flood waters could not penetrate. And the incident is not unique. In July 1959, a rain of fish was reported at Townsville airport in Australia.

Certainly, some falls have appeared to deny orthodox analysis. What to make, for example, of the rains of blood occasionally reported in medieval Europe? Precisely such an event occurred in Britain on the night of June 30, 1968. The bloody deluge, however, proved capable of scientific explanation. The red rain was found to be composed of fine sand picked up by dust storms in the Sahara and carried northward in the upper air to fall over Britain during a thunderstorm.

In Florida, it is not uncommon to see the ground carpeted by tiny little frogs during heavy rainstorms. One theory is that the rains cause dormant eggs to hatch en masse while another is the wind theory that says the winds pull frog eggs from the tops of ponds and they hatch in the warm rainy air.

Either way it is a bit disconcerting.

CHAPTER EIGHT: DEATH AND BURIAL

In the Midst of Life

At the funeral of a Georgia grandmother, held in Blairsville in July 1982, the preacher concluded a moving address with the words "We never know what is going to happen next."

Seconds later, a bolt of lightning struck the grieving grandson, Donald Metcalf. He was killed instantly.

From the earliest days of newspaper publishing, the press has dwelt with terrible fascination on circumstances of sudden and curious death. Human interest in the subject is timeless.

This chapter presents a modest catalogue of unhappy endings. For example:

A Judicial Error: While demonstrating how a revolver could have been used by the defendant on trial in a shooting case, Judge D. F. Sotomayor of a Tijuana court shot himself behind the left ear. He died an hour later. The judge had been under the impression that court officials had removed the cartridges.

Actress Killed by Press Cuttings: A pile of bound press cuttings and other material toppled onto Miss Eleanor Barry, aged seventy, a former actress, in the New York home she shared with her sister. Police said the house was filled with towers of books, newspapers, shopping bags, and assorted papers.

Baptism of Death: While celebrating the joyous ritual of rebirth at a river baptism in western Columbia, seven Adventists were swept away by strong currents and drowned.

Delayed Reaction: A Lewisham man died in an epileptic fit. The inquest heard how he had suffered from fits ever since an organ grinder's monkey jumped on him nineteen years earlier.

Undertaker Overcome: A fifty-year-old Turkish undertaker was killed when a tree branch he was cutting for a coffin fell on his head.

In 2014 there were two verified reports of people—thought to be dead—waking up at their funerals.

A ninety-one-year-old Polish woman, Janina Kolkiewicz, had been declared dead for eleven hours and her body sent to the nearby funeral parlor for preparation. She awoke, a bit confused, in cold storage. The embarrassed doctor told reporters that he had gone to the house after family members said she had stopped breathing. He checked her heartbeat, pulse, breathing and eyes and pronounced her dead, a bit prematurely it seems.

That same year, in the Philippines, a three-year-old girl was pronounced dead in the hospital Her distraught family made funeral arrangements for the following day. That was when one family member decided to remove the lid of the coffin to arrange the girl's body in a certain way and noticed the child's head moving. Her breathing was shallow and labored but she was indeed breathing. The girl had been sick with a fever but recovered and was allowed to go home with her family.

During the Victorian era, the fear of being buried alive was so great that some coffins—dubbed safety coffins—were outfitted with bells inside in case the deceased awoke.

The case of the Turkish undertaker illustrates the improbable occupational hazard to which unsuspecting tradespeople may be prone. Mailmen, of course, are very familiar with moments of apprehension as they approach houses known to contain dogs. There cannot be many postmen, however, who have been eaten by a shark. This was the melancholy fate that befell one Tongan islander as he carried out his chore, the circumstances, however, require a little explanation.

Most mail carriers dread the dogs on their route. But a postman on the island of Tonga had to worry about a shark attack.

Tin Can Island is the most remote of the Tongan group and has for many years operated a unique mail service. Until recently, letters were dropped to the islanders in sealed containers which were collected a mile offshore by swimming postmen. On one occasion, however, a postman was taken by a shark. Since that day, technology has transformed the islands postal service. The postmen now use canoes.

Sometimes the circumstances of a demise are so bizarre that they warrant extended treatment in the press: it almost appears as if the fates had conspired to arrange a fitting end for the victim. Consider, for example, the case of the badtempered golfer reported in 1982.

The man was an unpopular figure at the Sun Creek golf club near New Orleans. So many members had shied away from him that he often had to go around the course by himself. He would hurl his putter into the lake after a bad clip, or smash his ball wildly in any direction after slicing or hooking a drive. After the smallest errors, he would curse at the top of his voice.

On one occasion in May 1982, however, the man was invited to join three members who were seeking to make up a foursome. For ten holes, his temper held and his behavior was beyond reproach. Then, on the eleventh tee, he sliced a drive awkwardly, the ball disappearing into a thicket. This was too much—the old rage rose again in his gorge. He ranted. He raved. He hurled his club against a nearby motorized caddy cart.

The club head snapped off on impact and the broken shaft bounced back. The jagged end pierced his jugular vein like a spear, and he died on the way to hospital.

Equally ironic was the very different case of a Polish emigrant to Britain, whose inquest was held in 1973. This man lived in terror of vampires.

A retired pottery worker, the man had come to Britain some twenty-five years earlier. At the inquest, his landlady said: "He thought vampires were everywhere. He used salt, pepper, and garlic to keep them away." A police officer went further, describing the man's lodgings as looking like "a real Dracula's Castle:"

> *In the room was a ritual distribution of objects as antidotes against vampires. There was a bag of salt to the left of the dead man's face, one between his legs and other containers scattered around the room. Salt was also sprinkled on his blanket. There was a strong smell of garlic in the room. Outside his window was a washing bowl containing cloves of garlic. From a book,* The Natural History of the Vampire, *I found that these things were some of the methods used as a precaution against vampires. Apparently it was a Bulgarian custom, but there was no evidence that this man had been attacked.*

So terrified was the emigrant of vampires that he had even stuffed garlic into the keyhole of his room. As a last precaution before he retired to bed, he had also placed a clove of garlic in his mouth.

The man choked to death on the garlic.

Unusual Undertakings

The melancholy responsibilities of the undertaker have conferred a special dignity on his profession, at least as far as outward appearances are concerned. Once in a while, however, even morticians have been known to let the mask slip and reveal their flawed humanity.

In January 1965, a seventy-year-old woman was knocked down by a car on a highway in Nashville, Tennessee. A bystander telephoned the police, who sent for an ambulance from the Madison Funeral Home. In Nashville there are several funeral homes that operate ambulance services; every crash victim is, after all, a potential customer.

Eventually, the Madison driver arrived, and at last the unfortunate woman was rushed to Vanderbilt Hospital. Her condition was critical.

A slightly more dignified image of the motorized undertaker is provided by this advertisement, placed in the Waterloo *Courier* of 1925. Ed Kistner may not have been much of a poet, but clearly his heart was in the right place:

Ed Kistner is a very kind-hearted man,
To him you can always appeal.
He goes and gets his corpses at very high speed
Riding in his big automobile.
Should you meet with death some dark night you feel
And want an undertaker
Ed Kistner will be at your home very quick
For he goes in his big automobile.
No matter how dark the night may happen to be
Just telephone Ed Kistner and he will be there
For he has light on his big automobile.

A hint of eagerness in the verse, perhaps, but fittingly lugubrious. The following year, the Valdosta Times, another local American journal, carried an interesting personal ad shedding further light on the pioneer days of the small town mortician: "This is to certify that I, Henry Rains, who was accused and arrested on a charge of selling poisoned whisky to W. A. Curry, undertaker, was found not guilty, because it was only embalming fluid which he asked me to bring him, and not poisoned whisky. I am making this statement to vindicate my name."

Since those early days, the grander extravagances of the American way of death have become celebrated worldwide. In 1971, for example, the newspapers announced that the first high-rise mausoleum was to be built in Nashville, Tennessee. The building was to be constructed in the shape of a cross. It would rise to some three hundred feet and be twenty stories high with each level carrying seven tiers of crypts. Occupying less than an acre of land, the mausoleum would provide sixty-eight thousand burial places.

High-rise mausoleums may be fairly commonplace by now, no longer possessing the power to amaze. (In 1929 the *Times* startled its readers with the headline: "An Aerial Garage—Parking in the Skies!" The article went on to describe the first multistory parking garage in America.) Besides, no sooner had readers got used to Tennessee's extravaganza than Louisiana capped it with the world's first drive-in mausoleum.

The Point Coupee Funeral Home offered mourners the ease of viewing their dead relatives without leaving their cars. Visitors simply drove in and told the attendant the name of the loved one. Immediately, the dead relative beamed out through a 7-foot (213-cm) drive-up window, displayed in an open casket and illuminated by blue neon light. The owner of the home said that people liked the relaxed atmosphere of the place so much that he had already rented it out for special occasions.

During heavy flooding, it is not uncommon for caskets to become unearthed and wash away from their supposed final resting places.

You would expect no less from the state that features drive-through daiquiri stands!

That was in 1977. Only one year later, came the crunch. "Will the Crunch Replace Cremation?" asked the *Sunday Times*, picking up on the latest American innovation in decorous death. The aim of this grisly form of burial was to reduce the body mass without cremation. To begin with, the corpse would be frozen rock solid by cooling in liquid nitrogen. Next the frozen body would be pulverized by an automatic hammer into tiny chunks of bone, head, etc.

What could be more horrible? The final stage could be more horrible: in order to remove all traces of body fluids, "the particles are reduced to five percent their original weight by freeze-drying."

How cozy the coffin by comparison. Sharon Morrison, manager of the Rocky Mountain Casket Corp. in Montana found coffins so appealing that she began marketing them as articles of furniture that could be kept around the house until required for their final purpose. Her "furniture caskets," made of three-quarter-inch knotty pine and fir were made available in 1974. The fittings, though, were extra, allowing the coffins to be converted into such items as wine racks, drink cabinets, gun racks, billiard-cue racks, and "rustic coffee tables." The inventor of the convertible coffin was attorney Willy Von Bracht, who entered a local sports contest in a coffin toboggan of his own devising. However, he was well beaten by his own one-year-old son in a rocking chair on skis.

Interestingly, the Rocky Mountain Casket Corp. was by no means the first company to market furniture caskets. The *Strand Magazine* of 1894 illustrates a precisely similar product called the coffin cupboard.

Even creepier was the sight witnessed by many Louisiana residents in 2016 when heavy rains caused terrible flooding throughout the country. The heavy rains affected low-lying cemeteries the most and caused caskets to rise up and float around the park until the waters receded.

Similar gruesome occurrences occurred previously in the state during Hurricanes Rita and Katrina.

Not everyone lives in fear of their own demise, however. One woman, Christine Farman, held her own funeral party in July 1979. The sixty-four-year-old grandmother told reporters: "Like most families with old members we only seem to meet these days at each other's funerals. So I thought I'd hold my own funeral party while I am still around to enjoy it."

She sent out invitations far and wide. Relatives turned up from places as distant as Canada. In fact, so many arrived that she had to hire out the village hall to accommodate them. It was wonderful: "Now I'll die happy," she said.

One person who missed the festivities, however, was Farman's seventy-eight-yearold husband, Percy. Percy overslept.

"He's a bit of an eccentric," explained Farman.

Remarkable Requests

When Henry Cook, a prominent farmer, accidentally fell beneath a tractor, the doctors advised an operation to remove his left leg, just below the hip. While he was coming out from under the influence of the anesthetic he learned that his relatives had made a remarkable request on his behalf. Believing that the injured man's soul might suffer if his whole person were not buried in hallowed ground, the relatives ordered a fine copper casket, 3 feet (91 cm) long, 14 inches (35 cm) wide, and 10 inches (25 cm) deep to be prepared. It was lined with silk and in every respect other than size exactly resembled any other funeral casket. The leg was duly deposited in the casket, which was sealed airtight and properly disposed of. And so, long before his allotted span of years ended, Cook already had one foot in the grave.

The leg burial was a request of relatives. In other cases, those facing death have registered extraordinary last wishes on their own behalf. Take the case of Sandra West, aged thirty-seven, a Texas millionaire, who died in March 1977. It was her desire to be buried in a lace nightgown in her favorite Ferrari. The request caused considerable controversy and came before the courts in April of that year, when a judge ruled that her wish should be granted. And so, on that May, the extraordinary burial took place in San Antonio, Texas. As requested, West was laid to rest "with the seat slanted comfortably."

A more modest wish was registered by Kenneth James, a bachelor schoolteacher from Tower Hamlets in East London. His will stipulated that there was to be no funeral at all. His ashes were to be inconspicuously deposited "in any convenient dustbin for refuse collection in the usual way." James died in May 1977, but his will was only published in

Complete Recovery Expected

Much improvement was shown in the condition of Diamond Joe Sullivan today, according to a physician's report, and his complete recovery is believed assured. When attendants report him completely out of danger, Governor McRae is expected to fix the day of his execution.

—Little Rock Daily News

September. The witness had not, of course, read the will, so they did not know about his last request. In the event, his ashes were quietly buried, with no relatives present, under a hydrangea bed at an East London crematorium.

"We did not know of his wishes about the ashes," said a spokesman. But at least James was buried with anonymity.

Among all the bizarre requests that have been made, however, there can be none that surpasses that of André Tchaikowsky, who died in 1982. Tchaikowsky was an immensely gifted concert pianist (though no relation to the great Russian composer). And yet, the pianist's true ambition in life had been thwarted—he had always wanted to be an actor. Tchaikowsky died at the age of forty-six and asked that after his death his skull should be given to the Royal Shakespeare Company for use in future productions of *Hamlet*.

After checking with the Home Office to make sure that it was not illegal, the task of removing the skull was left to the undertakers in Oxford. A partner in the firm told the press, "Apparently he had a lifelong ambition to be an actor." The skull was later delivered personally to the Royal Shakespeare Company, wrapped up in a box. "We're somewhat bewildered by the whole business," said a spokesman for the company. "We'll store the skull away for the time being. As it happens, the company has no plans to stage *Hamlet* in the near future."

Unquiet Graves

In August 1982, the newspapers carried a macabre report from San Salvador, where a man's body had been illegally exhumed by his own relatives. It appeared that a lottery ticket seller had arrived at the dead man's house to ask why he had not claimed his prize of $40,000. Further comment is hardly necessary—it is not hard to picture the frenzied excavations, the desperate scouring of pockets, but the ticket was not found.

Graves have often been disturbed over the centuries by occult practitioners, and body-snatching cases have made regular appearances in the press since the celebrated affair of Burke and Hare in 1828. William Burke was tried for participating in the murder of sixteen victims whose corpses were destined for the anatomist's table of a certain Dr. Knox, who needed subjects for dissection. William Hare, Burke's accomplice in crime, was granted legal immunity for testifying against his companion.

The trial was a sensation, perhaps the first of the great nineteenth century crime blockbusters, and the public was as ghoulish in their interest as any modern crowd. "No trial that has taken place for a number of years past has excited such an unusual and intense interest," recorded the *Times*. "All the doors and passages to the court were besieged at an early hour before daylight, and it was with the greatest difficulty and the utmost exertions of a large body of police that admission could be procured for those who were concerned with the proceedings."

No details were spared to readers, of the lugging of corpses and the doings to death, though reports were couched in the cumbersome language of the early nineteenth century courtroom. Of the death of Mary Paterson, for example, the *Times* faithfully recorded that Burke allegedly "murdered Mary Paterson or Mitchell by placing or laying his body or person, or part thereof, over or upon the breast or person and face of Mary Paterson, when she was lying in the said house in a state of intoxication." The prosecution then went on to charge that "by the pressure thereof, and by covering her mouth and nose with his body or person, and forcibly compressing her throat with his hands, and keeping her down, notwithstanding her resistance, did suffocate or strangle her."

William Burke was hanged in 1829, in front of twenty-five thousand people in Edinburgh, and his infamous name has survived in the verb to "'burke"—meaning to smother or suppress. Hare, his accomplice, got off scot-free.

To counter quite justifiable fears of being buried alive, our forebears devised a number of ingenious contraptions. At the mid-nineteenth century cemetery of Frankfurt-am-Main, for example, a room was set aside for corpses; strings were attached to the fingers of the bodies and these were connected to warning bells. A certain Count Karnice-Karnicki devised a graveyard apparatus that consisted of a tube, a sealed box, and a ball which lay on the chest of the deceased. At the slightest movement, a signal was set off above the ground, a door in the coffin sprang open and light and air were admitted.

In 2012 in the United States, it was discovered that grave robbing, a longtime despicable act by the desperate to cash in on the wealth of the deceased, had taken on a new class of thief. Meth heads, or those addicted to methamphetamine, had resurrected the practice out west in order to fuel their high.

These drug addicts would steal absolutely any little trinket of value and try to sell it for their next high!

As late as 1926, the *American Mercury* recorded that "a telephone and electric lights have been stored in the mausoleum in which the body of Martin A. Sheets, stockbroker, was entombed. Sheets asked before his death that his tomb be so equipped that he might have opportunity to talk with the outside world if he should awaken in it."

The *Burial Reformer* was issued in Britain from 1905–14, specifically to press for improvement in burial customs. Renamed *The Perils of Premature Burial* shortly after its inception, the magazine exposed such cases as the Accrington Sensation of 1905, when a certain Mrs. Holden, aged twenty-nine, was laid out as dead and prepared for entombment; the undertaker noticed a slight movement while completing his task and revived the woman, who survived.

The magazine published a limerick popular at the time of the controversy:

There was a young man at Nunhead
Who awoke in a coffin of lead;
"It is cosy enough,"
He remarked in a huff,
"But I wasn't aware I was dead."

The macabre experience of being buried alive was granted to Michael Baucom, aged twenty, in 1982. Baucom was kidnapped, forced into a coffin and then buried under a Texas oilfield near Santa Fe. For four days he lay there in his underground tomb, with a little water, bread, and a tube to breathe through. His parents tried to pay a $75,000 ransom, but the kidnappers failed to turn up to collect the money. The police, however, tracked them down and freed the kidnap victim, who survived.

CHARLIE CHAPLIN'S VANISHED CORPSE

Charlie Chaplin, the world's best-loved comic genius, died on Christmas Day 1977 and was buried two days later in a little cemetery overlooking Lake Geneva in Switzerland. He spent his last twenty-five years in the nearby village of Corsier-sur-Vevey, where the comedian maintained a mansion. Throughout the world, newspapers published fulsome tributes to Chaplin's career both as actor and film director. His loss was genuinely felt.

And then, in the spring of 1978, while the tributes and anecdotes continued to flood in, a quite fantastic story broke. That March, press reports from Lausanne announced that the body of Sir Charles Chaplin had vanished overnight from its grave at Corsier-sur-Vevey.

The cemetery was small and square, surrounded by a low stone wall. It stood at the end of a narrow lane on the edge of the village; the comedian's grave lay close to a wall near an avenue of tall, dark cypresses. It was just one among some four hundred tombs mostly belonging to local people and marked by modest headstones and simple wooden crosses.

"The grave is empty. The coffin has gone," a police official told reporters. At the Chaplin mansion in the village, a

Silent film comedian Charlie Chaplin's body vanished from the Swiss cemetery where it was buried.

member of the domestic staff commented: "Lady Chaplin is shocked. We all are. We can only wonder why—why should this happen to a man who gave so much to the world?"

Swiss police instituted a search and Interpol was brought in. Local people offered details that, in retrospect, might have alerted them to what had happened on the fateful night. One man said that shortly after midnight he had heard a noise like that of a pickaxe from the cemetery.

But who would want to steal the comedian's body? A number of theories were advanced in the days that followed. Since there had apparently been no ransom demand, one possibility was that the body might have been taken by a group of fanatical admirers. Frederick Sands, an author, had written a book about the Chaplins that referred to the comedian having once expressed a wish to be buried in England, the country of his birth. The investigating magistrate contacted the writer who told police that letters had been sent to him protesting about the burial in Switzerland. Had admiration for Chaplin really attained such heights that it amounted to cult worship?

Other theories concentrated on the fact that Chaplin was Jewish. A Hollywood report alleged that the body had been removed because Chaplin was buried in a Gentile cemetery.

For a living film star to be kidnapped would be sensational enough. But Charlie Chaplin's corpse? The essential weirdness of the affair mystified both press and public,

Then, a few months later, came the news that the kidnappers had been found and the body recovered.

The culprits turned out to be two East European motor mechanics. The men, Galtscho Ganev and Roman Wardas, had obtained political asylum in Switzerland some time earlier from other countries.

And the motive: it was ransom after all. Amid all the distressing press speculations, the Chaplins had had to keep silent to protect the police operation.

Briefly outlined, the kidnappers' story was that Wardas had got the idea for the body theft when he read a newspaper report about a grave-robbing case in Italy. He was unemployed at the time and going through a difficult period: "As a result I decided to hide Charles Chaplin's body and solve my problems." Wardas was the "brains" behind the scheme (if such a term can be applied) and Ganev, his accomplice, was merely the muscleman.

They took two hours to dig out and remove the coffin from the Corsier cemetery. Then they loaded it into the back of an estate car and drove it just 15 miles (24 km) to a cornfield at the eastern end of Lake Geneva. Wardas knew the spot because he had often gone fishing there. It took them an hour to dig a new grave. They inserted the coffin, took photographs, and filled the grave in.

The two men waited for several weeks before telephoning the Chaplin family with ransom demands. At their trial it was revealed that they had used threats of violence against the family to try and secure a deal. Geraldine Chaplin, the comedian's actress daughter, had taken the calls because Lady Chaplin had been traumatized by the whole affair. Wardas had threatened to shoot Geraldine's younger brother and sister unless his demands were met.

But the kidnappers were, in reality, a sorry pair. They kept lowering the amount of the ransom. The police had been tapping the Chaplins' phone since the grave was robbed. The kidnappers announced that they would give instructions for the final ransom demand at 9:30 a.m. on a certain morning. That morning, the police kept watch on more than two hundred telephone kiosks in the Lausanne area—Wardas was nabbed.

Wardas confessed at once when arrested but would not reveal the identity of his partner in crime. The Bulgarian was quickly found, however, by checking up on the Pole's acquaintances. In fact, both "brains" and "muscle man" alike were so incompetent that when required by police to guide them to the burial site, they could not pinpoint exactly where they had hidden the coffin. Police officers had to use mine detectors.

The pair were convicted of disturbing the peace of the dead and of trying to extract a ransom. Wardas was sentenced to four and a half years of hard labor, while Ganev was given a suspended sentence of eighteen months.

It had been a bizarre affair, as bizarre as any of the films that Chaplin had made. It had also been deeply distressing for the family. "Instead of the love that centered round my father in the house, there was fear and threats," said Geraldine Chaplin.

And the corpse? For all the supposed desires of Chaplin's elusive cultworshippers, the comedian's remains were reburied in the same little cemetery at Corsier-sur-Vevey. The event had taken place quietly and before the trial. Only a few close friends and relatives were present at the simple graveside ceremony on May 23, 1978. As before, the body of Sir Charles Chaplin was laid to rest among the sad cypresses and modest crosses that overlook Lake Geneva.

But this time, the tomb was specially lined with concrete.

Chapter Nine: The Ultimate Taboo

Who Shall We Have for Dinner?

In 1973, there was a chronic meat shortage in Chile. One morning in February of that year, a laborer returned from an all-night drinking spree and delivered to his wife a 10-pound (4.5-kg) slab of meet. How had he come by this unexpected delight? He told her he had been offered the meat at a bargain price in a Santiago street market. Without further ado, the wife set to work preparing a more than usually meat-rich stew.

The couple found that they had more meat than they needed, and the thrifty housewife sold some to her next-door neighbor. This woman's suspicions were aroused, however, by the appearance of the meat. The skin and hair looked strangely human.

The two women took a package of meat to their local police station. Their fears were confirmed—it was human flesh. Appalled by the discovery, the husband then admitted that he had not bought the meat, but had found the package lying on the ground.

A few days later, the trunk of a human body was found in a sack on the road to one of Santiago's cemeteries. It was soon proved to have belonged to the same individual as the meat—they formed part of the dismembered corpse of an unknown murder victim.

Cannibalism inspires a horror perhaps exceeding any other human practice. Although the unwitting cannibalism of the Santiago couple is by no means unique, human flesh

Cannibalism has been practiced throughout history. For some, it proved dominance over an enemy. For others, it was a matter of survival.

has generally been consumed for one of two reasons: to obtain perverse satisfaction or to allay the peril of starvation.

There is an area in which the two motives meet—that of ritual cannibalism. Historians tend to believe, for example, that the Aztecs originally consumed the flesh of their enemies out of sheer necessity to supplement a low protein diet. The practice then developed ceremonial overtones. The same may be true of certain African tribes and of New Zealand's Maoris.

The *Illustrated London News* of May 21, 1842, contains a curious account of a Maori man arrested for being drunk and disorderly. The man turned out to be a Londoner born and bred, who had been kept a captive of cannibals for many years.

His name was Joshua Newborn, aged about twenty-five, and his "swarthy visage was tattooed like a native of New Zealand"; he had a strange tale to tell. Eleven years earlier he had been a boy on a whaler sailing the southern seas. The crew had fallen into the hands of the New Zealanders and had all been captured and eaten by them. He had been reserved until last, but his life was spared when he agreed to live among them. Accordingly, he was given some narcotic and underwent the painful process of tattooing.

He lived among them for ten years altogether, often joining them in their battles with neighboring tribes and attending banquets in which prisoners were killed and eaten. Eventually, he managed to escape and make his way home to England, where he was exhibited as a Maori chieftain at places of public amusement:

> *A police constable of the N division stated that while on duty at a late hour on Monday night he heard an extraordinary kind of yelling in Hoxton Square, and proceeding to the spot, found the prisoner dancing about, and disturbing the neighbors with his wild and terrific cries. The prisoner, who was drunk, instead of desisting and going away as desired, set the witness and other constables at defiance, and after a violent resistance was lodged in the station-house.*
>
> *Sergeant Lambert said that he was exceedingly violent at the stationhouse, and vowed vengeance against the constable who took him there, threatening to feast upon his heart and "lick his chops with his blood"; and during the greater part of the night he appeared to be dancing his war dance in the cell, screeching at the top of his voice.*
>
> *The prisoner, whom the New Zealanders had named "Moika Makoura," the meaning of which he stated to be "The Tattooed Spirit," now expressed sorrow for his disorderly conduct. He very seldom drank spirits, but when he did, he said it made him quite wild.*

One of the most bizarre cases of recent years occurred in California in July 1970, when two men were stopped by highway patrolmen near Big Sur. They had only been apprehended for a minor traffic offense. One, however, confided: "I have a problem. I'm a cannibal." He then confessed to murdering and eating a social worker.

The most notorious murderous cannibal has to be serial killer Jeffrey Dahmer, who killed, raped, and dismembered seventeen boys and men between 1978 and 1991.

Dahmer would regularly cruise gay bars and convince someone to come back to his apartment, where he would drug them and kill them. He would then dismember the bodies and boil pieces to separate the flesh from the bones. He had a real fascination with skeletons and skulls and tried to keep as many as he could as souvenirs.

The boiled flesh? He ate it. He would also freeze and refrigerate some of the organs to eat later on.

Dahmer was sentenced to life in prison but was soon murdered by another inmate in 1994, two years after being sentenced.

Cannibalism practiced out of sheer necessity comes into a very different category. Who can say with any confidence that they would not, if reduced by hunger to the pit of desperation, partake of human flesh? How can anyone, indeed, expect to understand the madness of starvation if in good health and well fed?

A German-born aviator put these questions directly to reporters in 1973. He was the pilot of a mercy mission aircraft that crashed in the Canadian Arctic wilderness. He was carrying three passengers: a pregnant Eskimo woman, her nephew, and a twenty-seven-year-old British nurse. The Beech craft airplane crashed in a blizzard while on a 500-mile (804-km) flight to take the nurse and her patients from Spence Bay to Yellowknife. David, the Eskimo boy, was suffering from suspected appendicitis, and his aunt was in premature labor.

The nurse died in the crash and the Eskimo woman two hours later. Both of the pilot's legs were broken. He and the boy managed to live for twenty days on a meager supply of corned beef, sugar cubes, salt, and soup. The boy built a shelter, provided firewood, and gathered lichens and mosses. As their condition weakened, the pair ate the frozen drugs in a medical bag and shared a 1-inch (2.5-cm) piece of candle.

After twenty-three days, the boy died of starvation. At first the pilot wanted to die too, but then the will to live reawakened. "I made a soup of lichens, no more than a spoonful," he said later. "I knew that since I could not get enough lichens to live, I could not make it to the lake—12 miles—to get fish. I needed food to fill the gap. From here on I think it is clear to everyone what I did. I'm still trying to forget this and probably will never succeed."

The pilot began to eat the body of the nurse and lived to survive his ordeal. He was rescued after spending thirty-two days in the frozen Canadian north. He admitted to his cannibalism soon after he was found by the Royal Canadian Mounted Police. At the inquest that followed, the nurse's parents stated that they bore no malice towards him.

The Hanover Vampire

Nothing more revolting has been disclosed in the history of crime than the career of Fritz Haarmann, forty-four, known as the "Hanover Vampire."

Haarmann, a black-marketeer, was brought to trial in Berlin in December 1924 and sentenced to death for twenty-four murders out of the twenty-seven charged against him. All the victims were young men. His young accomplice, Hans Granz, was also ordered to beheaded, but the sentence was subsequently commuted to twelve years of penal servitude. The details of Haarmann's atrocities were so dreadful that even the popular press glossed over certain aspects. Reynolds's *Illustrated Newspaper* noted: "Suffice to say that Haarmann was a sexual degenerate, that he lured the boys into his house, and after giving a sumptuous meal he would praise the looks of his young guest. Then, later, in a room upstairs, the crime was committed.

"The end was always the same. Haarmann held his victim down and killed him with a bite in the throat. The monster's teeth held tight until the young life was gone."

Fritz Haarmann, the "Hanover Vampire," killed his victims with a bite to the neck. And that was the least of his crimes.

Even here the horror did not end. After World War I, many Germans lived close to starvation. Haarmann, like other black-marketeers, traded in meat of uncertain origin. The *News of the World* reported: "All his victims were between twelve and eighteen years of age, and it was proved that the accused actually sold the flesh for human consumption. He once made sausages in his kitchen, and, together with the purchaser, cooked and ate them."

For most of the ten-day trial, Haarmann was impassive. Once, the proceedings were held up so that the accused might smoke a cigar. It happened while the mother of one of the victims was giving evidence; Haarmann was in such an obviously nervous state that the judge asked him if he needed anything. Haarmann requested a cigar to soothe his nerves and an usher was ordered to bring one.

The accused did not deny the murders—he was in no position to do so, for the evidence brought against him was overwhelming. But he claimed that they were all committed while he was in a state of trance. Hundreds of people had come in and out of his house quite safely. It was only when the irresistible urge came upon him that he went out and roamed the streets of Hanover to bring in a victim. He could not say what followed; he was not conscious when the atrocities were committed.

Afterward, he cut up and disposed of the bodies of the boys. Their clothes were put on sale in the shop of an accomplice. Skulls were thrown into a river that ran in the back of his house.

Haarmann had taken extraordinary risks, and it was astonishing that suspicion did not fall on him earlier than it did. The whole of Hanover was alarmed by the disappearance of so many boys. How had he escaped detection? Some believed that Haarmann's meat trade was looked on indulgently by the police. Certainly, he had some connection with them; he acted as a police spy, and influential officials may have sheltered him when he first came under suspicion. Several members of the police force admitted that they had received gifts from him. In general, he was known as an obliging and pleasant-mannered man.

For the first few days of the trial, the evidence was given behind closed doors, "being of too revolting a nature to find a place anywhere outside medical books," as *Reynolds's* put it. The monster's account of how he disposed of the bodies, however, was delivered in open court. Nearly two hundred witnesses gave evidence, mostly parents and relatives of the murder victims: "There were scenes of painful intensity as a poor father or mother would recognize some fragment or other of the clothing or belongings of their murdered son. Here it was a handkerchief, there a pair of braces, and again a greasy coat, soiled almost beyond recognition, that was shown to the relatives and to Haarmann. And with the quivering nostrils of a hound snuffling his prey, as if he were scenting rather than seeing the things displayed, did he admit at once that he knew them."

If Haarmann was a psychopath, what of Granz, his accomplice? The man emerged in the trial as a sinister figure whose motives were shadowy. Cynical, callous, he drove the victims into Haarmann's room and he clearly knew what was happening there. On one occasion, Haarmann was going to release a victim—Granz drove the boy back to slaughter.

There were some clues to Haarmann's own mental condition; in particular, a driving hatred of his father seemed to have been a dominant obsession. Haarmann did not, however, use insanity in his defense. On the contrary, he implored his judges not to send him to an asylum. He had been confined to prisons and mental hospitals during his earlier days and did not want the experience repeated. In fact, time after time, he appealed that the trial be ended quickly so that he could be put to death.

The close of the trial was sensational. A fanatic had sworn that he would shoot the murderer as soon as the sentence was pronounced so that no opportunity for clemency could be exercised. Every member of the public who came into court was carefully searched for weapons. Expecting a fatal shot at any moment, the judges were protected by a row of policemen watching for the slightest movement in the gallery. Though the threat heightened the courtroom drama, the fanatic did not make his attempt.

Concluding his own address, Haarmann pleaded:

> *Condemn me to death. I only ask for justice. I am not mad. It is true that I often get into a state of which I know nothing, but that is not madness. Make it short, make it soon. Deliver me from this life which is a torment. I will not petition for mercy, nor will I appeal. I have made things easy for you gentlemen; make them also easy for me. I should like to add that the police have done everything possible to clear up the affair. At first I denied, but they started rather roughly with me, and that I cannot bear. Afterwards the situation became clear to me and it is still absolutely clear. I thank you gentlemen.*

When the sentence of death had been pronounced, the doomed man asked that the following inscription should be inscribed on his tombstone: "Here rests the mass murderer, Haarmann."

He also expressed a desire to pass "one merry evening" in his cell. His last meal should consist of coffee, hard cheese, and cigars, after which he would curse his father and regard his execution as his wedding.

Blood Pudding

During World War II, large amounts of human blood were collected from those British citizens willing to donate it to help casualties. So much blood was in fact given that there was something of a surplus.

Scientific advisers to the government, meanwhile, were worried about the nutritional requirements of the civilian population. They put forward a scheme to use the blood surplus as black pudding for distribution on the war ration.

The Ministry of Food eventually rejected the idea. Indeed, the proposal was only made public in November 1969, when Dr. Magnus Pyke was giving a lecture to the Royal Institution in London on the subject of food and society. Pyke had himself been a scientific adviser during the war and cited the rejection of the scheme as a "striking example of the way in which food taboos can hamper good nutrition."

It was interesting, he noted, that the British were quite prepared to consume each other's blood by vein—but considered taking it by mouth to be a variant of cannibalism.

The Andes Survivors

As far as the outside world was concerned they were dead. Stranded in a wrecked fuselage high amid the Andes, the members of a Uruguayan rugby club had a choice: they could starve to death or eat the flesh of friends whose bodies lay scattered in the snow. Sixteen chose to live, and their tale is as heroic as it is bizarre.

On October 12, 1971, forty-five Uruguayans left Montevideo for Santiago in a twin-engined Fairchild. Most were young men and members of the Old Christians rugby club. Their team had finished second in the Uruguayan league and was now off to play a match in Chile. After the game there would be a few days of skiing in a Chilean mountain resort. Some members had mothers and sisters with them. They were looking forward to the holiday.

The plane belonged to the Uruguayan Air Force, and the flight was delayed because of bad weather in the Andes. But the following day, the aircraft set off again. High above the mountains, however, a blizzard set in. The plane hit an air pocket, jolted, and went into a dive with its engines screaming. And for months that followed, all that the world knew was that the aircraft had disappeared.

Onboard the plane, however, an appalling ordeal was beginning. The aircraft plunged some 3,000 feet (914 m) in a matter of seconds. Snowy crags were glimpsed not 6 feet (1.8 m) from the wing tip; and then the plane dived again, smashing against a mountainside, its tail plane wrenched off to careen down the slope.

"People who failed to get their seat belts fastened were simply swept out of the hole left when the tail broke off," a survivor named Inciarte later recalled in a *New York Times* report from which much of the following material is drawn. "Blood spurted all over me, people were screaming, and I could smell fuel and the cold air gushing in from outside, when suddenly with one big bump we came to rest."

The aircraft lay amid mountains rising to 21,000 feet (6,400 m), in a place as desolate and remote as Antarctica. The pilot was dead in the wreckage. Sixteen others lay dead or dying around, including all the women passengers.

Staggering to their feet amid the carnage, the twenty-eight survivors felt the bite of the sub-zero temperature. But at least they did not perish overnight from the cold, for they had with them the warm skiing clothes they had brought for the projected holiday. Those clothes, and the fitness of the young club members, were to prove crucial in the months of suffering which followed.

There was also a transistor radio, though it had no batteries. The only surviving member of the aircrew declared that batteries were stored in the tail. It was 2 miles (3.2 km) away. An expedition was mounted to retrieve them, but they were found to be too heavy to move. Instead, the radio was taken to the tail and attempts were made to rig up a transmitter for signaling distress. After many days of struggling with numb fingers, however, the attempts failed. Nonetheless, it did prove possible to set up a receiver, and the group was able to listen to radio broadcasts from Montevideo.

Powerless to guide or inform, the Andes survivors heard of search parties and rescue squads scouring the mountains for signs of the vanished aircraft. With every day that passed, the hopes of the searchers grew fainter. And at midday on October 21, the survivors heard the news they were dreading. The search parties had been called off. The Chilean Mountain Rescue Service announced that attempts to find the plane would resume during the spring thaw. No one, it was thought, could have survived in that temperature and in that terrain.

And yet the group had survived. At one end of the wrecked fuselage, the partially destroyed cabin offered some

In 1972, a Uruguayan Air Force plane crashed in the Andes mountains, killing many and leaving survivors with a difficult dilemma.

insulation against the bitter cold. At the open end, an assortment of partitions was erected. The aircraft had settled into the snow up to window level. It was hardly snug, but it sheltered the group against the worst of the elements.

Covers were ripped from seats and converted into blankets. Some people slept in hammocks composed of cable and cord. Others slept on metal plates laid at an angle against the wall; they developed sores on the backs of their necks from lying night after night in the same position.

They slept as close to each other as they could to keep warm, and the restless tossing of one might graze the chapped limbs of another. But there were few serious quarrels. Team spirit, as much as fitness, played its part in sustaining the club members during their long ordeal.

At first, the survivors had tried to eat snow for water. Severe cramps ensued from the cold. Later, aluminum sheets from the plane were propped up to provide a solar melting device. Snow piled up on top warmed and dripped into bottles placed underneath.

Such solid food as had been stored in the aircraft was gradually exhausted however. And as the days passed, and the pangs of hunger grew stronger, the decision to consume flesh from the bodies of dead companions was taken.

The choice was not easy to make.

Not everyone chose to accept the decision. One survivor, Numa Turcatti, considered the toughest and fittest of the group, suddenly lost heart in the business. He was given food but he hid it and threw it away when the others were not looking. Turcatti simply let himself die.

But those who had determined to survive at all costs took precautions as sensible as those applied to the fitting out of the fuselage. Strips of flesh were cut up and left to hang until ready for consumption. A rationing system ensured that each corpse should last the survivors five days. Nobody feasted with relish. The flesh was consumed in small pellets to minimize the ordeal of chewing. The madness of starvation remained close at hand, and everyone experienced hallucinatory dreams of fantastic banquets. Once, the survivors drew up a list of the best restaurants in Montevideo to while away the hours of numb despair.

On the 29th , a fresh disaster struck, further reducing the group's number. An avalanche bore down on the aircraft, wrecking their living quarters as tons of compacted snow churned through the fuselage. Nine lives were lost.

From the outset, group members had made small foraging expeditions when taking the daily trips to the radio in the tail. All movement was slow in the thin air, but sometimes an excursion brought a reward. One big find was a packet of 170 cigarettes fallen from the plane as it burst apart. After the avalanche, however, the survivors felt more strongly than ever how precarious their existence was; it was clear that someone should at least try to reach help.

Three men were selected for the expedition. To equip them for the intense cold, the group pried felt covers from heating tubes in the aircraft, fashioning them into bands to be wrapped round the men's bodies.

Of the three who set out, one turned back after three days in order to save rations. The two who continued were Parrado, a burly rugby forward, and Canessa, a third-year medical student who had become the group's doctor. On leaving, Parrado had promised: "Before Christmas I will have you out of here."

The feat the two men accomplished was an epic of endurance. With their improvised clothing, they scaled heights that had not been attempted before by fully equipped mountaineers. "We had no idea where we were going," Canessa recalled, "but with the aircraft compass we had to get there. Chile was to the west and we would go there whatever happened. So we started those unending days of travel—intense cold at night, intolerable heat at midday. We rationed the water and food and I said: 'If we don't walk so far, then no food for us.'"

It was Parrado, however, whose extraordinary stamina and determination proved the most enduring. Toward the end he was carrying his companion.

On December 20, a forty-four-year-old cattle hand from San Fernando was tending his herds in the foothills of the Andes. He heard faint cries from across the River Tinguiririca, a rushing torrent that carves its way through the mountains' lower slopes. On the other side he saw what seemed to be two tramps. The roaring water drowned the men's shouting—he had his cattle to look after and night was falling. He shouted that he would return the next day.

The following morning, the tramps were still there, and still the torrent muffled their cries. The cattle hand threw over a piece of paper and a pencil attached to a stone. The message they hurled back read: "I come from the plane that crashed in the mountains. I am Uruguayan. We have been walking like this for ten days. My friend is injured. There are still fourteen injured people on the plane. We have to get out of here quickly because we have nothing to eat. We can walk no more."

The cattle hand rushed off to find help, but it was midnight before patrols reached the pair.

Meanwhile, there was jubilation in the wrecked fuselage. The survivors had learned by radio that Parrado and Canessa had got through. The arduous discipline of maintaining the aircraft had been abandoned. The last remaining cigarettes had been rolled into huge cigars.

By the afternoon of December 22, most of the survivors had been rescued by teams of mountaineers supported by helicopters. Those who first reached the scene were astonished to find human limbs scattered outside the aircraft and strips of flesh hanging inside ready for consumption. Neither Parrado nor Canessa had spoken of what had passed in the mountains. Indeed, the earliest press reports described the survivors as having lived on lichens. The experts, however, knew that this could not be true. The survivors were too fit and too lucid. The full story emerged only later.

Bad weather prevented the last survivors from being taken off the mountain until December 23, the day after their companions. It is not hard to imagine the mixed euphoria and anxiety of the little group huddled in the lonely hulk during that last night in the Andes. All were freed nevertheless.

In total, the Uruguayans' ordeal had lasted seventy days. But Parrado had kept to his promise—he got them all out by Christmas.

GLOSSARY

anecdotes—Short and often amusing stories that are supposedly true.

apartheid–The former law in South Africa that was based on discrimination and separation by race.

apocalypse—The end of the world as we know it.

aviation—The act of flying a plane, helicopter, or hot-air balloon.

exhumed—To dig up something that was previously buried, usually a corpse.

fanaticism—Devotion that goes beyond the normal and is excessive.

humility—To be modest and not look for credit or recognition.

insemination—The act of fertilizing a female of a species for the purpose of reproduction.

obsession—To be passionately consumed by something.

meditation—The process of relaxing to the point where one feels detached from the anxieties of real life.

synthetic—Something man-made.

truncheon—A short bat or club normally carried by police.

FURTHER READING

Books

Birdsong, Leonard. *177 Dumbest Criminal Stories.* Orlando, FL: Winghurst Publications, 2015.

Hunter, Max Mason. *True Paranormal.* Amazon Publishing, 2016.

National Geographic for Kids. *Ripped from the Headlines: Real-Life Stories You Have to Read to Believe.* Washington, DC: National Geographic Publishing, 2014.

National Geographic for Kids. *Ripped from the Headlines II: Real-Life Stories You Have to Read to Believe.* Washington, DC: National Geographic Publishing, 2015.

Websites

Guinness World Records
http://www.guinnessworldrecords.com
Listing of world records and the attempts to break them.

Ripley's Believe it or Not
http://www.ripleys.com
A collection of strange but true facts and stories.

Strange Facts
http://www.strangefacts.com
Pages and pages of fun, weird, and bizarre facts.

INDEX